The Oubliette

The Oubliette

A Novel

By GRANT WHITE

RESOURCE *Publications* · Eugene, Oregon

THE OUBLIETTE
A Novel

Resource Publications
An Imprint of Wipf and Stock Publishers
199 W. 8th Ave., Suite 3
Eugene, OR 97401

www.wipfandstock.com

PAPERBACK ISBN: 979-8-3852-4875-9
HARDCOVER ISBN: 979-8-3852-4876-6
EBOOK ISBN: 979-8-3852-4877-3

VERSION NUMBER 040925

To my children: Roxie, Jaxson, Adalynn, and William

That which is named the Universe is not to be understood as coterminous with base outer space. Mathematics has taught us that spaces themselves can be compact and yet, in a very real sense, infinite. Shakespeare codified in the popular imagination that, in certain instances, nutshells can also contain infinite space and potentiality.

—Constantin Delargy

Contents

1

The Stealing Away

So near to the end, this story in the limit is effectively at the end itself. It is of course an objective fallacy for both humans and spirits to assume that closeness to the end implies any sort of reduction in ontological value. These ideas have been put down many times, and here I do it again. And these words redound forever. My name is Ithamar, and I record here the open secret that, while time is real and well and good, time is also equally valuable at all points. This is a necessary consequence of infinity existing at the same time as value existing at all. This missive will be written as if I had an audience. Given infinite time, which I shall have a few things to say about anon, and only a finite number of archived lives and available readers, the probability tends in the limit to one. The concept appears again to be a solid one, that these words will be read, but if not, I have an audience. And more importantly, at least in my case, I have a duty.

—Unfinished story fragment by D.L.B.

LIFE WAS ON HIS mind that night.

The gravel he was kicking under his feet was certainly not life, but he had been told that the rustling in all the reeds in the ditches, as he walked, did constitute life.

One set of inanimate things was dead, the other set fairly teeming with activity and life. An I was rounding the bend, the moon was orange cheese, and the conglomeration of atoms that formed the body of Daniel Lawrence Blythe was chemically compromised.

As he walked, there was a delay in his senses. Movement, then lag. Movement, then lag. He had decided to leave the keys with Eric. He could walk back the next morning, pick them up, and drive the truck off his lot.

Eric's mother owned the lot, in truth, but it was thought of as Eric's, because the poor woman never really checked in on the doings of her son. There had just transpired one of the regular, but not terribly raucous, parties at her house—hence, the reason Daniel decided he would walk back to his rental house just a quarter mile away.

It was approximately eleven o' clock in the relevant swath of the United States. His feet crunched in the gravel. The cicadas were droning. The air was humid.

He saw the outlines of swaying trees and the effect of the orange moonlight was such upon them that they looked like they belonged in an old cartoon with a low frame rate.

This conglomeration of atoms is having a hard time expressing himself, he thought.

They—all of them—professed to party, but none of them experienced the height of hedonism. He did not particularly enjoy strong drink himself, but he could be coaxed to partake when he was in the company of his friends—especially when the alternative was to ruminate alone. Eric had been there, and Jason Schubert had shown up after having been away with his cousins for most of the summer. In fact, much of the usual group was there, and the local gas station had almost certainly noticed an uptick in cigarette sales for the week.

He managed the used bookstore in town: Porter's Books. It was a cursory business propped up by cursory money in a dying municipality—or arguably one that had never lived to begin with. Nobody demanded, and nobody gave. He could have made no sales of any books, and he would still have a place to stay: his eight-hundred square foot rental house, which suited him just fine. The rent was nothing to his father, who would have put up should Daniel come up dry any given month, and this is without mentioning that the landlords of rural Arkansas are not known for being cutthroat.

He had all the books in the county. He had no woman, which was not a victory for him. And he had his thoughts. But on the night in question as he returned home, his thoughts seemed to be more self-referential than normal.

He patted his pocket to make sure the key was in. Ten more minutes over there, and I wouldn't be able to get through the door, he thought, assuming I could fit the key in the keyhole.

Close door. Collapse. Wake up tomorrow. A Sunday. Store doesn't open until 1 pm.

And I can live one more day. Which returns us to the subject of life.

In one of Arkansas's rural summers teeming with raccoons, cicadas, dogwood trees, and honeysuckle, with bats flying overhead, preying on the multitudes of vampiric mosquitoes that Sylvia's shapely white legs seemed to attract (so she often said and even had she not, it was rather apparent), Daniel was drunk and knew in his heart that all of these seemingly beautiful things were nothing but illusions, billiard balls—nothing but cascades of electromagnetic waves.

It wasn't even a problem that animals killed each other for sport and for sustenance, though that was perhaps a topic for another embarrassing drunken night. For what was the death of one compared to the death of another and the blood that was shed? It could be written as a connected dot diagram on a sheet of paper which is itself cellulose and so on and so on. The very media which explain reductionism of life are themselves reduced in an infinite regress, except that there is no infinity.

So, that's even worse, he thought. His foot stumbled and kicked an especially large puff of dust. Somehow, even though infinity is terrifying, that it's *not* infinity but still very large numbers may be even worse, because it means it eventually runs out and saturates the universe. It fills itself up with self-referential (like me) blather until it reaches critical mass or when life functions cease.

Why did he matter? What did it matter? (He realized that away in the distance, an owl hooted.) Why did it matter that he felt good? He did feel good. He realized he felt jolly—precisely as much jollity as could fit into several glass bottles. It seemed that Eric and Jason felt good, too.

He thought back to when he was a child, afraid to walk outside at night for fear that a coyote would always be there to nip at his heels. Once a cat had taken a swipe at him through some tall grass near his house. He could remember screaming running to the safety of his front porch.

3

He passed one house that had a single lightbulb switched on at the front porch, casting a sickly yellow glow. Moths performed a macabre dance about the bulb, spending their summer night—perhaps their last—throwing themselves into the buzzing miniature sun.

Eric and he had barely talked that night. Daniel's attention had been primarily fixated on Sylvia, whose presence always made him feel achingly aware of his own age, of the uneventful story that had been his own twenty-nine years.

Twenty-nine years. Gosh, by the time his own father was twenty-four, he had already had a wife and two children, with a magnificent (compared to Daniel's current lodgings) two-story house only three years in the future. As it stood, Sylvia was the only one he could have considered becoming Mrs. Daniel Blythe, and, because of that tenuous hold, children seemed about as likely as encountering a chimera in these woods. She was beautiful, and he admired her, but he didn't like the fact that she could slam down bottles of beer because women weren't supposed to—just then he checked himself as he walked, chiding himself that he had no right to impose any values at all on anyone.

He was staggering, veering off the macadam, surrounded by crane flies, great horned owls, imported bushes, and he was the chiefest conglomeration of atoms of them all.

Was not his chemical state evidentiary that he was merely chemicals? In some states of affairs, he could express himself well, but in others, his bodily form staggered, his head swirled, and his lips numbed. In some scenarios, atoms formed rigid lattices, and in others they were like free-flowing collapsing piles of sand. In all cases billiard balls clacking around in an uncaring void. Children with Sylvia—he hated himself for thinking this, but wasn't she merely that, too?

He was coming up to his house. No, it couldn't be the case—and yet Sylvia couldn't be the exception, either.

It came down to the fact that he could not have her for these reasons. The thoughts—only electrical impulses in a wrinkled mush of cells—swished around his addled head, which would be sore tomorrow. He was ruined. The way he thought of the world was reductionist, and he lived in a paradoxical cycle of needing others to make life less monotonous, yet barely believing that others (or himself, for that matter) were anything at all.

She would never understand him, would only recoil from him if she knew. He wrote a poem about the feeling once, before even knowing Sylvia, only pining for the woman who would one day be his wife:

I'll do, if all's written in a top-down scroll.

We'll have, if my Weltanschauung's under control.

It called to mind the season in his life, in his late teens, when he began to wonder if time was real. Was it truly the case that the future was unwritten, or was life just that which had gotten itself pinned under an immutable block of spacetime, everything preordained? How he had moved on from such tormenting thoughts, he could only guess, but he knew he could entertain the idea in his mind casually without his stomach knotting and the small of his back dampening anymore.

The top-down scroll in the poem was what he thought of as a certain type of preordainment; he wanted to be able to move freely within the reality afforded him, but didn't it also need to be the case that everything stuck, that everything would matter and be recorded in a great scroll?

And you might say, he thought, that God was the great writer of the scroll, but he and God were not on speaking terms.

Yes, this moving arrangement of atoms, forming vast chains of organic molecules, is having a difficult night of it, he said to himself. If he had been sober, the night would have been beautiful. Life was rustling and teeming (whatever it actually was)—enough so that his attention would probably be able to appreciate it before the reductionism in his brain set in again.

He had reached his front porch. With clumsy fingers, he wrestled his keys out of his jeans pocket, and, not without poking at the wrong spot a time or two, managed to get the key in the hole, and turned.

Being eight hundred square feet, his house was essentially one large room with a bathroom tucked away to his left. There was the couch   a relic from his parents' old married days, a gift from their friends—that would be his bed for the night. He was too tired and drunk even to turn on the light. Staggering to the couch, he plopped on it and was asleep within two minutes.

An hour later, he awoke. He turned on the lamp next to the couch and checked the clock: fifteen past midnight. All his fatigue and foggy-headedness seemed to be gone. Daniel briskly waved his hand in front of his face in the paltry lamplight, finding that his eyes tracked the movement with as much resolution as the normal state of affairs. How had he metabolized everything so quickly, he wondered.

"No, I'm going to feel it again later. I have to," he grunted to no one in particular. He shifted his weight to one elbow and gingerly lifted himself to a seated position on the ratty couch. The blanket and pillow fell away to the floor.

Then it hit him—the combined weight of everything that had tossed around in his head that night. The past ten or so of his twenty-nine years had seen his brain move from one topic of infinity (or vast numbers) to the next. Sylvia was unreachable, and, the sad truth was, were he to, odds against odds, reach her, his own thoughts would force him into a state of doubt that she was even a thing to be grasped at all.

So, really, he had no friends. The living beings with which he conversed were automata who were unaware of their tenuous place in the cold, uncaring order of things.

And so only he, Daniel Blythe, knew the secret? It was the same old round, over and over again. I don't have that much clout, he thought. Please, remember that you don't have that much say over anything. It would be the most supreme form of arrogance to suppose otherwise.

When he was young, he had developed a certain turn he could take in his mind, a certain well-worn pathway that, were he to traverse down it, would end with him wanting to have always been nonexistent. It was the infinity turn. Many a night had ended up with him sleeping at the foot of his parents' bed on the futon, because he would tentatively creep down the stairs with a "I had those thoughts again." The "thoughts" were (he was always ashamed to admit this to himself) that Forever terrified him. Daniel would hit the groove, the turn, in his mind and feel the violent wrenching of being propelled forth through eternity. Even in a benevolent heaven in the arms of Jesus, which was what he had been raised in, there was no end. This prospect was enough for him to want to clench his eyes shut and wait for something different to take hold of him—but there was nothing different. Life, reality (were they different?) seemed to be structured according to the maxim that eternity underlay everything.

The thoughts would often capture Daniel when he awoke in the wee hours of the morning when a horror of great darkness fell upon him.

God, I want you, but not like this. It goes on forever and ever, and I don't see an alternative, but could you tailor-make my eternal resting place to be one in which annihilationism overtakes me? But then what was the point of ever having lived at all? So, I return to being desirous of living and existing and writing my name on what I perceive to be reality, but somehow

I want a non-existent compromise between existence and finitude. And so, since I can't resolve this impasse, I doubt the premise: God must not be there, and I am merely running my mind through the useless grooves that found themselves in organic beings with no reference to the outside.

So on this particular summer night that had just shifted over to the morning of a glorious Sunday, Daniel was experiencing the infinity turn in his mind, which saw him pleading God not to exist at the same time that he was pleading nonexistence not to exist; he was mourning the loss of Sylvia, the beautiful girl he had never had and never would have due to the reductionist disease that had long ago besieged his thoughts; he was commenting on himself being nothing but a alcohol-affected cluster of organic molecules that somehow were dead and mindless but also felt good and jolly with his friends, who were either illusions and so he had a solipsistic view of the universe, or who were fellow addled clusters parallelly living out the "life" of their atomic bonds until chemical processes failed them; and he was painfully aware, in the dim of his glorified shack underwritten by his far-more-successful father, that his twenty-nine years had been a waste, and that his talents—particularly intelligence and articulation—were squandering themselves in a shop that slung pulp shlock.

These processes culminated and slid past one another in his head. Then Daniel vanished from the Earth.

The Arkansas crickets continued their nightly chorus as usual with one less listener.

2

The Bean

The age was that of the Other Man. Science had reached a level to which it was not unfeasible to imagine lifting off from the terrestrial realm and making contact with civilizations unknown.

The disciplines of science and imagination were at quite an overlap. Having conquered totalitarianism in Europe, the Western Hemisphere moved to conquer distant yawning gulfs of space itself. Everyone knew that lightspeed was the ultimate absolute barrier. Everyone knew that to have a conceivable mechanism by which to traverse the stars, some fanciful propulsion method would need to be developed.

They scribbled their fancies all over blackboards in universities across the United States. And since matter can never be lost or gained, the Cipher still existed–the Cipher detailing such theoretical hyperdrives dwelt as chalk specks on the floor to be swept up into the dust bins as new ideas took their place.

By the year in which this story takes place, one could accurately say that a fever for interstellar flight was literal. It was overflowing the waste dumps–had permeated the nation from the waste dumps upward.

None of the preceding accurately captures the way the spirit of the age had engrossed the imagination of children, for with the idea of space comes the idea of life.

For me, it had created this paradox, and, as all paradoxes can be, many popular imaginations, while believing the paradox, tried to refute it. The general sense that was on the wind was that there had to be intelligent life. There just had to be. For it was beginning to be seen more and more how intelligent the world was, and every so often a couple of oldsters came forward with the occasional odd story of believing they had been visited. It all coalesced into an age of space and life.

—Unfinished story fragment "The Cipher" by D.L.B.

DANIEL OPENED HIS EYES, and Sound itself became tangible. For he could not have really been seeing, he was hearing, and the sound itself—the pulses, the undulations—had no other recourse but to present themselves as waves and bellowing to his eyes. For surely his eyes were not really open. But as Daniel touched his eyeball with his fingertip to confirm this, the stinging, violating pain that one normally feels confirmed to him that yes, his eyes were open, but it would not be completely proper to say that what he was experiencing was sight alone. As his senses collected themselves, and as he became more aware, he decided that attending to memory would be something he would return to later. His intuition impressed upon him the idea that he needed to become familiar with his surroundings, for his surroundings were very alien.

The first visually-oriented detail that is easy to describe would be the coruscating colors—the kaleidoscopic pinks and blues and greens similar to the rainbow effect on an oil patch resting on top of water. These colors sparkled, dazzled, undulated. And as time went on in the future, Daniel would often find himself losing track of all time gazing at the patterns, though it did not occur to him immediately. Even later he was able to make the connection that the ever-shifting pigments and patterns were almost exactly like the phosphenes one sees upon a vigorous rubbing of the eyes.

It appeared to be a vast cavern. Later, he would find that it was not as vast as he thought. Billowy, syrupy, undulating walls, pulsating with sounds—inextricably linked with the sensation of sound as if it were a giant heart—beat irregularly, sporadically, causing these wave-like pulsations. And in the sea of colors there were no odors, nor no tastes to the air. Daniel was perhaps twenty feet away from the nearest fleshy wall. To his surprise, he realized he woke up (if he had indeed been asleep) standing. Could he move his legs? Though his whole atmosphere was one of pulsations, his body felt oddly rigid.

He could open his eyelids. That was the first immutable truth to which he could cling, though his sense of sight was confused with his auditory sense. He could move his hand. He looked down to find that he was still wearing the garments that he had had on before he blacked out—leather boots, blue jeans, and a short-sleeved, light green Oxford shirt.

Next, he tried testing his extremities. He wiggled his toes; he could feel the familiar bunching up and letting off of each muscle he decided to flex—hands, feet, legs. For the next few moments, his world consisted in firing his moveable body parts. That he was in a psychedelic, living rub of the eyeballs would have to wait.

But similar to one who is stiff and has not used his muscles in some time, Daniel found that it was difficult to bend his knees and to coordinate his body in all the complex motions of walking. He had to bend himself then quickly unhinge himself in order to get the looseness required. The ground was spongy and turfy, and it would not have been wrong to think that it was wet; however, there was no liquid. There were no drops; there were no puddles, just a squelchy, fleshy softness that reminded him of viscous, but dry, clay. The floor did give enough counter-force to allow him to walk as normally as he could, albeit awkwardly, as he slowly stumbled to the nearest wall. Up until this point, he had been moving in total silence (ignoring the discrepancies between sight and hearing and the troubling confusion of senses—maybe he was simply still drunk?) but as he reached out a faltering hand to the wall, wondering if he would be able to stabilize himself, he heard—seemingly through his hand itself—a distant basso profundo.

He jerked his hand back as if it had been hovering over a snake hole. He thought he let out a cry, because he felt his breath sharply exhale from his mouth, but he did not hear himself. The distant hum came louder and louder. Steeling up his nerve anew, he got his fingertips within about six inches of touching the wall. The profoundly low frequency was deep in his ears and vibrating his chest. But he could not find himself able to touch the wall—it repelled his hand like the wrong end of a magnet. He jerked his hand back to his side, and he found that his hand, cold and clammy, rested straight in an unnatural pose, as if his body had a neutral mannequin-like rigidity that it would return to if he was not moving. He wondered if he would be able to sit, or if standing was all he would be afforded to do. His hand was stiff with at his side as if he were about to perform a crisp military salute, and his legs felt like marble columns.

The silence had returned.

Daniel walked again over to the wall, his hands not swinging, his arms rigid. He stiff-walked near the wall and found that as he crept forward closer and closer, the wall opposite him became more vigorous in displaying its swirls and sparkles and scintillations. There was no gap between what was appearing in his eyes and what was throbbing in his chest. The sound returned louder and louder as he took each faltering step forward, feeling imbalanced without the use of his arms. What had happened to his arms? Was he not able to free them?

Finally, Daniel covered enough ground. He panicked, fell forward, letting out a silent cry (he confirmed it was silent this time) as he felt that he was about to fall and not be able to catch himself with his arms.

He fell forward, and his head rested into the soft wall.

Any fear for his pain or safety was immeasurably drowned in the explosion of sound that enveloped his whole body, including his eyes. The universe was nothing but sound-sight. For the first time, his sense of smell presented itself: the colors smelled as they sounded and as they sighted. If he had been able to produce his own noise, he would have been screaming from the very gulf of his being, from the place where his not-being gradated into his being. His sense of touch-sound was limited to feeling and hearing his head plastered into the fleshy side of the cavern. But really, none of that existed anymore. It was all sound—sound—sound. An eternal din. A demon's trumpet blast swallowing the universe.

Dear God, he thought in his mind, thankful that he had some amount of mind left after touching the wall. Dear God, if only I could die to make this sound go away. It won't go away. He found himself detached from his body; he was only mind. Only mind, only begging anything—anybody, the forces of the universe itself to stop the noise. The laws of nature themselves—if only they would remove this sound. He was nothing but a giant ear, and he was being destroyed and torn up into shreds—shreds of pulsating oil slick rainbow ribbons on the wall. His arms—he wanted nothing more of it—the sound—he wanted to resolve into the elements from which he came if only to escape the sound, the sound, the sound, the sound, and then finally he got a little better and felt a little bit more like an I again, got a little less expanded. He found that he was able to open his eyes again. But weren't they open already? Or were the phosphenes leaping from the pulpy barrier into his own rattled head?

While the sound was still rather loud in his ears, it had subsided enough to allow him to regain control of himself. He found he was lying in a fetal position with his back to the wall. He realized what had happened: he had stumbled forward and caught himself with his head against the wall. Who knows how long he had lain there, staying in that position as the drumbeat of Hades, overthrowing and yet enhancing all senses and all intelligence, had slipped by and rolled over him like a storm cloud?

Now that his ears and his head were away from the wall—at least by a few inches—Daniel noticed that his mouth was intolerably dry. What was wrong with his body? And though he had not begun to process where he was and what had happened to him, the events of the past three minutes had so utterly shattered him that he could do nothing but close his eyes.

When he awoke the answer was in his mind.

Whatever the sound was, it emanated from beyond the wall and, in an asymptotic manner, the closer a part of him was to touching the wall, the louder the sound was.

That was perhaps the second truth, he realized, to which he could cling.

Daniel was standing in a giant bean—a bean with undulating walls of psychedelic swirls. Even to describe his surroundings adequately would require dimensionality that was not available to him. But for the sake of description allow yourself to imagine a gigantic, ovoid-shaped hangar two hundred feet long lengthwise and perhaps one hundred feet in width. He was situated at the end of the semi-major axis staring the full length (practically speaking) down to the other far chamber of the bean.

As his strangely behaving eyes adjusted to their new surroundings, Daniel estimated, using his own body height as a rough standard, that the ceiling (were it to remain still and form a true planar surface) was twenty feet above him, and he was on the spongy ground, gently waving, having slowly and ponderously arisen to his feet again.

While it was a bean in shape, for some perhaps non-Archimedean or non-Euclidean geometric reason, the angles that the floor made with the walls did not afford themselves the ability for Daniel to test whether gravity behaved the way he expected it to behave. However, at one point Daniel did try and found that he was rooted to the ground, same as on Earth. He found he was unable to walk up the walls and hang upside-down from the ceiling. And that was ultimately another question, he had to admit: was he removed from the Earth? The last clear memory he had before this was awakening on his parents' friends' donated couch, a bit astonished that his drunken feelings and disorientation seemed to have vanished. Then he remembered feeling the very familiar sense—that had waned considerably as he had departed further and further from being a child, but still felt exactly the same when it did show up—that he very well was headed for an infinity of existence after death. The angels formed a circle in space, and he propelled forward through the celestial hoop, deeper and deeper and wider and wider until his physical shoulders tightened and he had to pound his figurative chest with his figurative fist to dislodge the thoughts.

Then he found himself here in this large oval-shaped enclosure, almost mesmerized by the colors and swirls dancing on the walls.

While the walls were colorful, they were not particularly bright. There was no immediate source of light; the walls did not seem to supply them. No lamp, no sun, no fires, no candles—but the interior was bright enough. The brightness appeared to be an inherent property of the bean. When not oscillating, the walls were smooth with one notable exception, roughly halfway through. In fact, were he to have a measuring device Daniel would have found that exactly halfway (with infinite precision) through the enclosure there was a shallow trench cut in the floor running from one semi-minor axis wall to the other. The strips of wall that projected upward from the trench on either side, arcing upward to meet on the ceiling above were noticeably static compared to all other portions of the interior of the bean.

Given that it was an anomaly to the environment in which he was steadily acclimating himself, Daniel determined in himself that he would explore this trench. The entire odd, robotic process of activating his legs, compensating for his unusual balance, with his arms being curiously the most rigidly fixed portions of his body, began, and Daniel succeeded in walking over to the trench and, instead of a gentle kneeling motion, he crouched down to his knees brusquely and, since he had no arms in which to support himself, or to balance off his knees, he fell forward, only not crashing his nose upon the floor due to the fact that the trench was shallow enough to awkwardly cradle his body as when he was testing out the wall behind him. As he lay there, doing an internal check if anything hurt, he noticed that since his head was near the purported floor, the bottom of the trench was similar to a one-hundred-foot riverbed perhaps three or four feet deep, but with nothing in it, and entirely empty and irregularly carved as if dug by a shovel with uneven shuffle strokes. He further noticed that his head was near the floor and realized that he had not been lying for several minutes (as he had initially supposed), but he had been in agony listening to the thrumming and the pounding that was reverberating through his skull, just like a few minutes prior.

With immense effort, he wrenched his body off the floor and situated himself so that he was sitting cross-legged at the bottom of the trench, barely able to see over its lip. Daniel sat there in a daze, afraid even to let his mind wonder what was happening to him and where he was. Still seated, he held his arms out for balance, as if to steady himself from further accidents. And this conscious thought bloomed forth in his head: The first rule is to keep my head away from the walls and the floor.

3

After the Ellipsis

Minds connect with minds in the ether between thoughts.
An inquiring mind will find what it sought.
A true fetter between two conscious beings
Will open a sight-sense far beyond seeing.

—Poem by D.L.B., age eighteen

IF ELLIPSES COULD BE real, tangible objects (but of course, still nothing but billiard balls) instead of dots on a page, if ellipses could exist in real time, Daniel would have seen ellipses shoot through the air of the bean in which he found himself, because in his head he was completing thoughts that he was not sure he was even having, and words were present in his consciousness that did not seem to have a beginning, but only a middle. In that nebulous way in which thoughts behave, he was suddenly aware of another consciousness, and that consciousness was talking. And the talking had been going on for some time; it was not the beginning of a talk, but rather, he was plunged into the middle of a speech, and when he closed his eyes, which was the natural tendency of his eyes anyway, and when he listened to it, he almost felt that it was English that he was hearing. However, he was in actuality not hearing English words being spoken, but he could regardless understand everything perfectly.

"Do you think for a moment that you're unique? Do you think for a moment that this is some sort of chamber designed especially for you? I will tell you right now, indeed right now, this is not the case. You are in here—true. And I will make do with you—true. And we will get to know each other—true. The long cycle of days will be felt; you will feel them. You will feel the long cycle of days, and they will never end. They will impinge themselves on your very bones, and you will begin to see what I see and will begin to know my life; you will begin to know my reality, and you will suffer, and yet you will also experience joy, for it's in the suffering that joy can be felt in the binary juxtaposition of the two."

Daniel was still seated cross-legged in the crude trench exactly splitting the bean in half. Fear took hold of him unlike anything he believed he had ever felt before. What was talking? Where were these bizarre, foreign words coming from?

This was it, then. He was dead. He had asphyxiated on his vomit after having too much to drink that night. Or he had fallen off the couch and broken his neck, killing him instantly.

But did that hypothesis feel right? He glanced around with a stiff neck, surveying his confines. It was not a matter of whether his surroundings represented any traditional depiction of any afterlife. How were the living to know? It was whether he felt dead.

And I don't feel dead, he thought. He looked at the smooth strip of ceiling far above him, standing out all the more by the swirling colors avoiding it on either side. He glanced down along the curvature of the rippling walls, perhaps rounding the bend one hundred feet distant from each bank of the trench. There was something he had not taken in before. He shifted his body so that his shoulders were parallel to the trench and so that he was facing the far curve of one end of the bean. He moved to resting on his knees (not an easy feat with his arms nigh-immovable) so that he could better peer over the edge of the trench.

Near the far curve of the bean, too far away for him to be able to gauge the distance from him properly, but possibly thirty feet from the rounding of the ovoid, was a sort of dark alcove in the wall, level with the floor, that held a semicircular shape despite the turbulence of the walls.

No sooner did Daniel notice the alcove that an immense frog, approximately the size of a compact sedan based on his estimate of its distance away, hopped out of the hole and rested in front of it so that its hinged hind legs and feet barely broke the plane formed from the floor of the bean and the enclosure.

Somehow, Daniel knew the strange words he was hearing, and which were still going on ("Yes, I will not welcome you here, for you belong here despite the fact that you are useless and as nondescript as any other . . .") emanated from the frog. Whether the frog spoke through telepathy or some other means, Daniel was never able to determine, but he certainly knew that the frog employed no vocal apparatus to communicate and, as the long future went on, hardly ever opened his mouth at all.

"Oh, you are becoming aware, then, of me? I will apologize for the way I tend to ramble. Quite possibly, your awareness of me has just switched on. The Oubliette has that effect on its visitors, although I'm lying. You are its first and only visitor. I am not a visitor since this place belongs to me. It is my home and will only more so become my home as the eons march on."

Existence was ludicrous. He could not be dead, Daniel told himself. Bodily sensation—as limited as it was—did not enter into it. This was intuition. Daniel decided, as panicked and frozen by fear as he was, to adopt the hypothesis that he was—in the normal, unqualified use of the word—still alive.

But the chance was nonzero that he was entirely wrong and that he had died and was now experiencing a new mode of being.

And the eternal ages would roll on, no matter where exactly he was, and his greatest fears were finally realized . . .

He couldn't think of any of that right now. His surroundings were becoming too bizarre and at a speed that was hard for him to process. Could he talk? In the seemingly few minutes that he had been in the bean, Daniel had heard no sound other than the grating of hell that had occurred twice when he pressed himself too near the walls of the bean (though, curiously, he could sit or walk on the floor with no issue).

". . . must familiarize myself with my disembodied voice, friend, because it will be the only thing you hear, and I use that word figuratively, because sound waves do not always exist in my Oubliette. I'm afraid I don't know why, but it doesn't cause too much of a problem.

"Oh, I sense that you are wanting to speak to me! My friend, form the words in your mind that you want to say—speak them clearly as if you have a microphone inside your brain—and I will hear them."

Daniel complied with the frog, concentrating his muddled brain and scattered thoughts into words, surprising himself with his very first choice of sentence:

"Have you been monitoring my species?"

"No, but everything I tell you is a lie."

"Why am I here? Where are you taking me?"

"Everything I tell you is a lie, but you're here because I selected you to be here, and I'm really taking you nowhere. This is the destination that I intended for you."

"Why do you look like a frog?"

"I'm not sure the reason for your question. This is the form that I've always had from time immemorial."

"Are we traveling? Is, is this some kind of vessel?"

"We're always traveling. We're propelling forward through existence. Not necessarily through time, but we're existing and therefore we are traveling, scratching the On."

Daniel was flummoxed. He knew he could breathe, and he started to realize that perhaps the motion difficulties he was experiencing were related to gravitational differences between his usual environment and the interior of the bean.

Since he did not feel dead and went with the theory that he was still alive, all possible explanations had been exhausted. And the only one that was left in the bottom of the sack was this: he was in the custody of an interstellar (perhaps even an inter-dimensional) being. He was in the craft of an alien race so utterly foreign and so advanced technologically that the machinery and internal mechanisms completely escaped his notice. The incomprehensibly ear-splitting, universe-rending sounds he had encountered earlier were the sounds of the engines thrusting by some means of Einsteinian relativistic space-bending propellant traveling through empty space, and he would either be killed, sacrificed, experimented upon or worse. His twenty-nine years of life on Earth, unhappy years, had culminated in this—the story of his life, assuming such stories were truly written somewhere in a great cosmic repository or, as he put it in his couplet from long ago, a top-down scroll.

(Editorial note: The irony is not lost on me. People often do this. In fact, it is a sign of the infinite true yearning for God. That people do wonder if there's a book is only natural. I want the ledger to know and to be assured that there is such a book. In fact, without such a book, there would be no

meaning–there would be no beauty in it. —Quote by Ithamar in an unfin-
ished story fragment by D.L.B.)

He was one of the crazies, one of the people that would occasionally make the news and radio rounds—people that swore, would even swear with a hypothetical truth serum in their system, that they saw dark figures that could only be aliens. They saw elongated heads peering at them from outside their window at night or at the foot of their bed, or they witnessed bright lights and heard humming overhead as they drove their car down a dark country road. Only, for him, it had truly occurred.

Daniel had not counted on any extraterrestrial disrupter of his life assuming the guise of a giant frog. Were the familiar amphibians he had always admired in fact creatures that were relatives of this massive alien race, brought to Earth by some sort of panspermia?

Or were all his theories on everything, including the afterlife, wrong, and this was going to be reality from now on?

"Listen," he said. "Please listen. I know you can understand me. I don't know why, and I don't know how. But you need to listen. I am . . . I am nothing. I am nobody. There are other people, people of my type, people of my species, of my race, that would be better equipped to talk to you. If, if you mean peace . . . I mean, I want you to understand that I can offer you nothing. I am merely a lowly representative of my species—what we call the human race. (You probably know all about us.) I do not even have the power to direct you to important people. I could at best direct you to a local leader who could, in turn, direct you to someone higher up and so on until the proper person is reached. I'm not the one you're wanting. Please let me go. Please let me go. I can offer you nothing . . ."

Daniel experienced next the first of what he would call the Lapses. The Lapses would occur when he asked a poor question, or when he said something that he found later on was regarded as foolish. A Lapse consisted of a darkening of the bean's intrinsic light source, a lessening of the colorful swirls, and a sensation in his mind of time passing—long spans of time dur-ing which the frog was silent and immobile just inside his alcove, having waddled slowly and awkwardly backward through the opening. He would usually seat himself cross-legged in the trench.

During these Lapses Daniel found that he moved much more sluggish than before, when he dared moving at all from his seated position; he had no real measurement of time other than his internal clock, and not even his hair or his nails or his beard grew. While the contents of his first (and even

19

his second) Lapses are soon to be recorded, at least very limited aspects of them, it is important to note that as time went on in the bean, there was a clear ramping-up aspect to the Lapses. They grew longer and longer in duration, if a human's inborn sense of time can be trusted and no relativistic effects corrupted the clocks. Such a thing was never known—possibly not even to the frog.

During the Lapses, he would let his mind lapse into reverie, but with one caveat. There was a constant refrain in a certain distant corner of his mind of let it stop, let it stop, let it stop.

Before he found out the true meaning of the Lapses, and before he learned the purpose of his sojourn in the bean, Daniel would often scrape together in his mind any snippet of scientific concepts he could remember—speculative science, conjectural technologies. For instance, he could remember reading an article in some National Geographic something-or-other article about future deep space exploration theories, one of which was the purported need to put men in stasis, since space missions on the magnitude written about would require years of travel even at velocities approaching that of light. It was a theoretical venture, to be sure, since nothing nearing the sophistication needed existed in his time. He wondered if the Lapses worked like some kind of stasis, for they were like a reverie—a dream that simultaneously felt that much time had passed and very little time had passed. For when a Lapse ended, Daniel felt at the same time that he was just awakening and also that he had been acting for time out of mind.

The first Lapse ended, and the frog spoke. "I am listening and I'm aware. I'm aware that there are others—what you would call the chain of command. You're not special. I didn't choose you for any significant reason. I don't even have whims or reasons beyond your reckoning. Everything I do tell you is a lie. I don't want to speak to what you would call leaders."

"Why? What can I offer you? Are you going to experiment on me?"

"That won't be necessary."

"I can tell you anything that you need to know. I can even live where you're taking me," Daniel said.

"I want you to trust me that where I'm taking you is here. This is your destination," said the frog.

"Am I to understand that this is your planet or your home world?"

"Planets. Home worlds. Heavenly bodies of all types. Spherical rocks with satellites roped in around them, resembling macromolecules. All arbitrary. All arbitrary. Existence on your scale could have been anything else. In time, you will come to see that, too. But I have to ripen you to it first."

"I don't doubt it," said Daniel. "Fine. It's all arbitrary. Everything is a stand-in for something else. What I'm telling you is that your efforts are futile, for surely this endeavor takes time and expenditure of resources and effort that you are wasting on someone such as me, when you could be speaking to a great king or a great leader or president on our planet. You're not going to reach an understanding with my species if you keep conversing with me. I am trying to convey to you the idea that I don't have any sort of clout."

"I know," the frog said. "I don't care."

Then Daniel's stomach rolled in on itself. "So, you are going to take me away from everything I know, then."

"I'm not going to. I already have."

A gong reverberated in Daniel's head, although he was nowhere near the walls or floor of the bean.

"To what purpose?" Daniel asked.

The second Lapse occurred.

4

The First and Second Lapses

And it will have always been the case that thinking and not-thinking
are one, for all coalesce in the ultimate of ultimates.

—Lesser oracle of *le fils de la ruse*

Lapse One:

The interior of Eric's mother's house was a step or two away from being utter squalor. They were only in their twenties, after all. The least of the
offenses was the sink, which was stacked full of crockery, much of which
had food still caked to it. Ashtrays were ubiquitous throughout the living
room, and all inside the whole house miniatures St. Agnes mountain fitness
rest of the gang was tarrying Eric Daniel's were in the room through the
screen door, cicadas were droning on the night was taking on like gray blue
mid summer both of the men's shirt sleeves were rolled up. Cloth was sticking to their backs and life was while supplied with cigarettes and sweaty
drinks a trudge?

Say if Sylvia does come I'm gonna ask you guys to step out of the house
you know talking about eating take a walk or something there there's a trail
Mr. Watson next door kind of a trail through his property and takes you
out by the lake. Nice place to walk but I need the house alone for a bit

if you know what I'm talking about. Sloshing his mirrors in I don't even know if they're gonna come but if they do I get it. Starts turned for a bit she certainly was the kind of creature he could expect or could hope to spend his days on Earth with seemed that all the scientists of the day had wives children or they would write away the existence of meaning in their books. Sell them for a profit. Take the money home multiply the human race there was sitting there dens smoking a pipe bearskin rug on the floor. Which one was it was the what was the true scientist she could do nicely in fact he wanted to do for her it wasn't a one sided transaction . . .

. . . Yes, scientists would write away existence and meaning itself in their books, then sell them for a profit, take the money home, and, at appropriate times, multiply the human race with their wives . . . Pipes, smoking jackets, bearskin rugs, shot glasses, dinner with the Jacobsons, and life and reality were still illusory, billiard balls upon billiard balls . . .

Daniel shook his head, slowly in the enhanced gravitational field of his—yes, it would be accurate to call it a prison for now. How long had he been experiencing such a mishmash of thoughts? It was as if his thought-life was wafting in and out of dreams. Ideas coalesced, memories presented themselves, swirled with absurdity, and exploded forth in his head. It seemed that the images and suggestions of Sylvia were the most formed, so whenever his awareness floated over to thoughts of her, he tugged at them with all his might.

Sylvia, a veritable sylph. She of the golden, frizzy hair and the pale skin. It was a tremendous tragedy that he and she could not be together. Where was she now? He had been so close to her last night, if indeed less than a day had truly passed since he had been with her. Would she believe that he was in his current predicament, were someone to tell her? Would it be possible for the two of them to make it, despite his propensity to, like the scientists of his books, except with none of the actual training, write off human existence? Did scientists' wives blithely follow their husbands' pronouncements about life and the world, or did they provide a check on their wild imaginings? How could you procreate with someone, knowing that the consciousness produced in your offspring was a mere illusion? How could he be intimate with someone, aware that the physical sensations he felt were epiphenomenal offshoots of his having a bundle of wrinkles in his skull—all of which were billiard balls held together by the equivalent of electricity shooting through the air?

Sylvia. I'm here, and I am baffled as to what here is . . . but then again, I'm baffled as to what you are, too, if I'm honest with myself.

The alcove was still closed.

He was beginning to lose the thread. If he relaxed his concentration, his thoughts relapsed again into near-gibberish, akin to the oil slick rainbow of patterns swirling on the epidermis of the walls around him.

My friends would have the last laugh. What do I mean by that? Eric, Jason, others . . . I never let them know the full bounds of my despair—that in my deepest heart I doubted whether they were legitimate beings at all. Not that I was the only mind in the universe (though it certainly feels that way at this time), but that we were all equally lost—or were never there at all, it was better to say—in a wash of an alien, uncaring cosmos that spewed us forth, wound us up, and deceitfully allowed us to be constructed in such a way that we thought meaning was beneath every stone, that nebulae were found in every pile of twigs.

There was absolutely no reason why an alien spacecraft had to be built of metal and pipework. It all made dubious sense. This was some sort of living ship. Or perhaps he was merely in one infinitesimal chamber of a vast interstellar vessel, and for some unknown reason his quarters were flesh-like and organic.

Maybe the frog was merely some sort of avatar, a type of organic robot, and the extraterrestrial beings in command of the *Oubliette* had yet to (or never would) reveal themselves. It could be that in their survey of planet Earth they greatly misconstrued their data so that, to them, thinking from the mindset of one of the planet's inhabitants, a massive, talking frog to keep him company was entirely logical.

And I am rooted in this cell, and when I was a lad swimming in any pool, I would cry out from under the water for God to hide me away, and that is exactly what is happening.

If he could tilt his head just right and move his eyeballs to their extreme rightmost limit, he could barely make out the frog's alcove. It was as if a giant brutish eyelid had closed over the opening.

That's right. All I have to do is clearly speak the words in my mind and the apparent telepathic link between us is established.

"Where are you?" he screamed in his mind.

"Hello? Can you hear me?

The frog gave no answer to his mind.

Throughout the time Daniel had already spent in the *Oubliette*, it would not be accurate to say that he had experienced panic up to this point. He knew bewilderment, shock, disbelief—but not panic, merely because his brain almost seemed to be actively rejecting the sensory inputs he was receiving. It was then that he remarked to himself that the synesthesia he had had upon waking in the bean seemed to have settled, but, similar to lying in bed and being unable to pinpoint the exact moment he fell asleep, he would have been unable to recount exactly the demarcation between having sound-sight and having each sense back in their proper corners.

But he was beginning to panic now. Daniel was seated cross-legged in the bean's trench, barely able to peek over the rim, focused on the wall in front of him, scarcely able to move his body, and his only companion—one that he had barely traded words with—an alien frog-creature the size of a Volkswagen, was out of sight.

What am I expected to do here? he wondered to himself. He attempted to stand and found decisively that he was unable to muster the strength and coordination to do so.

More panicked thoughts were birthed. How long had it been since he had drunk or eaten? Was he going to stay rooted in this position until he died of thirst? Or would his alien captor—surely dependent on water itself, unless it was not organic—eventually supply him with his hydration needs? Once again Daniel wondered exactly how long he had been in the bean . . . and then his attention was engulfed with more memories . . .

He could remember sitting in the living room of one of his teachers. The occasion was Wednesday night Bible study and one of the dads—Mervyn Hollis was his name—delivered a devotional that night head to head delivered a devotional perhaps in eighth grade we know we could never have Erin trinket was the focus of the occasion . . .

Concentrate, he told himself.

"God is eternal," Hollis said. "He has no beginning; he has no end. Said bourbon. I don't know about you." He was a big man, shirt sleeves. Always rolled collar always disheveled sweat always sticking his shirt white shirt to his importantly frame . . .

Concentrate, he said again. He picked a point on the wall, seemingly ever-moving, but he needled his eyes on the point and shaped his consciousness into it.

"I don't know about you, boys and girls, but it's easier for me to imagine eternity moving to the future forever than to fathom no beginning. I personally just can't imagine that, but that's what it says in the Bible," he said, pointing to nowhere in the Bible in particular.

"No beginning. Can you imagine? Can you even wrap your head around it?" He chuckled.

"So what are we? Really, what are we? We are said to be eternal. We are said to have a destiny. In heaven, or, sadly, in hell. We're eternal." He gave a dramatic pause. "And yet we have a beginning."

Chuck DeGraaf raised his hand and asked, "Didn't we exist as souls in heaven before we were born?"

Hollis leaned his bulk against the stone mantle with an I-was-anticipating-that expression on his face. "There's some real good theories behind that. There are some real good theories. You know, let's think about that. If we existed as souls in the mind of God and were in heaven, in paradise, before we were born—as if God selected us to be given to our parents—the question comes: Why would God bother to send us to Earth in the first place if you're already in paradise?"

Tucker Howser said: "Because he wants to test us".

To which Pete Kirk nodded his approval and added: "Right. This is like the testing ground. The Proving Grounds. See if we got what it takes."

Hollis suddenly had the look of a man who knew that his topic was failing and the floor he commanded was being usurped, as pockets of kids (there were perhaps ten in all) began to turn to one another and pick up aspects of the concept.

Why bother even making proving grounds at all?

Why did he do it?

We all already existed.

Why not leave well enough alone?

Because that's just the mind of God, and we really can't fathom it.

But couldn't God make it so that we would just love Him and serve Him without falling or sinning?

He can't do that fairly without giving us the proving ground.

Which is my point exactly.

What do you mean by fair?

But there's nowhere in the Bible that says . . .

Brenda Gildan raised her voice, an edge to her tone, and made a gesture like an umpire declaring a runner safe.

"Guys!" she exclaimed.

A hush more or less came over the crowd. Hollis looked gratified that someone had gotten back control for him. He resumed: "My question was, guys, what are we? There has been some good discussion over the past couple of minutes, but no one has given me an answer. Let's get ourselves back into it. I think we have a beginning. Let's say this to be accurate. We have a beginning. We have a beginning in the earthly world, whereas God doesn't. So are we eternal?"

Lapse Two:

The gray-blue of evening pushes through the shades. Soon, the color will resolve into night, but in these brief moments I look out through the slit between the blinds and the window jamb and see the neighborhood splayed out before me. The night-birds are calling as I wrestle within myself with the thoughts that my father and mother will die someday, and I will have to carry on their name alone. I both want heaven and eternity to be here now in the gray-blue and to be far off in the ambiguous future. Here in the light, present, past, and future are one as I wish the world goodnight with troubled eyes and furrowed brow and pray that the world will be more sensible in the morning.

Another reverie had occurred, this one lasting from the birth of the universe until its death. A kalpa, as he recalled it being named once, the pitiable dance of rebirth and re-death. It felt like he had been in the *Oubliette* for centuries, somehow. Surely, everyone he had ever known was dead, and they died—returned to the elements from whence they came—never knowing what had become of him.

All because I asked the frog the reason why it was taking me from everything I know and (I suppose) love, he marveled. It has this power over me. Like using a cattle prod on an unruly cow, it can plunge me into these spells and then hole itself up in its little alcove when I am acting uppity. But I have all the time I could ever need.

He was now in a sort of trance, and he was facing the iridescent wall of his bean prison. No hunger pangs or the unmistakable feeling of thirst ever came upon him, although his mouth remained perpetually dry. A part of him chalked those anomalies off to the unfathomable technology of the makers of the bean-ship. He imagined that he was inhabiting a non-entropy zone, and perhaps such base things as food and water were not needed here in the bean.

Or he could have been horribly misinterpreting everything and had been dead all along, but he willed himself to concentrate anew. There was still no need to entertain that hypothesis without further proof.

Although the feeling of long ages passing and him never seeming to decay or have basic organic needs was not insignificant . . .

The memory of Mervyn Hollis and his ill-conceived devotional was by no means the only brain activity he had had during the First Lapse (he would eventually stop counting them), but, other than flashes of Sylvia and hints of the night back in Arkansas when he was taken from her (not that she would necessarily feel the same sense of loss as him), that memory was the most well-defined. And even that threatened to be overtaken by the oil slick gibberish (he started to conflate the two things in his mind, for one was a good metaphor for the other) at multiple points.

Daniel could remember, even all those years ago, being puzzled by the point of Hollis's little talk. It had seemed to him elementary that musings on any direction of infinity were difficult for the mind to grasp.

Even in the ensuing years, as he became ruined, as he inadvertently corrupted himself by assuming his reductionism (but wasn't he obligated to face the truth of reality?) he never worried himself about the—as he thought—leftmost side of eternity, the idea that something or someone could not have a beginning. Over time, he came to reject the notion entirely—a necessary consequence, he thought, of reductionism. Things began only, and time with them.

He was seated, and his legs were bent in an awkward way—he was not a flexible twenty-nine-year-old—his feet resting on the bent knees of the opposite leg. Daniel himself never had heard this term, but he was assuming what other people-groups called the Lotus Pose. His spine, as always in the bean, was rigid. His eyes were unblinking and unfocused. It was as if he had a television screen on the wall, except instead of the snow of static, it was the comforting and familiar pink and green oil slick colors and swirls.

I'm going to be here forever, he admitted to himself. This is how I will die. I put off believing it until it was too late. I may have already died. Yes, I'm dead, and I'm unhealthy in my mind. And while I'm not physically in torment, my mind will assume the torment of eternal ages with only a finite amount of material upon which to chew. I may sit here locked in this rigid position forever, and in my lifetime, whether it is still ongoing or completed, I was or am only a finite being. The world I know may be collapsing down to an infinite decimal point to wait in the space beyond space until it decides to call forth a reiteration of its former glory, but my reality is here.

Oh, God.

It was like a dream, because he could simultaneously feel vast stretches of time, and yet sense unmistakably the urgency of now. And while he remembered that he had thought the words "Oh, God," the next thought he could remember having was that he had been contemplating music. And the memories came with it . . .

"Mom?"

"Yes, Daniel?"

"Is music ever going to run out?" She played the piano.

She patted his head to reassure him. "No, I don't believe it," she said. The thought had clearly never occurred to her before.

"The reason I asked that is because there are only a finite number of notes, and everything starts to sound the same after a while." He was sitting at the round kitchen table cluttered, as always, with books and crayons with their wrappers ripped off, pencils, toy cars and crumbs never to be wiped off. His mother was never able to hide her franticness; she never mastered the veneer of the dutiful housewife in control of her stewardship.

I'll have plenty of time to recontextualize all my memories, he realized, staring at his television screen of fleshy interstellar swirls, then recontextualize that and, even though in theory, just like the music I was wondering about, I could stretch this on and on, and while it might technically be different, it really won't be.

Was it truly novelty if, working from a finite set of building blocks, the only way to generate new pieces was to compose longer and longer ones? At some point the music became self-referential—all things did. Even utter noise would repeat itself.

Though it used to, the thought of music having only a finite number of meaningful combinations did not bother him at this point in his life. He had made peace with the finitude. Thinking back over his life during the kalpa, he remarked to himself that he was never without an obsession about infinity—whether it be the lack of infinite music, infinite words in books, or similar things. And while he had ever managed to go about his duties and life fairly well (despite the fact that he was an abject failure and waste of talent) beneath any calm facade he presented was always the roiling current of his uneasiness with the way the world was splayed out.

One kalpa ended and the next kalpa began. Where was that frog? He had the sense that the frog was not really rooted in its little alcove frog patient as he was would be able to while he was sitting there frozen, staring at the wall come over and slice his throat with what didn't matter. Something he could conjure up something slice his throat and then he would die.

Concentrate, he told himself. But his stomach knotted somehow despite the stasis he was in. We knew he wasn't going to be free assuming he was hell in hell and he died he would just go down to the next tail and the next tail on this never ending cycle. Never ending cycle worlds are living and dying, blossoming withering outside of this Oubliette outside of this bean. Like a fast motion slide reel played in school have bean plant the frame rate was so fast that almost appeared to be sprouting a stalk and leaves and flowers, then pods then desiccating in real time, except for the fact that there was a bit of jerkiness inherent in the motion is mind knew that this motion wasn't truly realistic.

Focus. You are losing yourself, he thought.

Now he was back to where he had started. He could remember lying in his bed as a young boy. In a way, he was thinking of the opposite problem. He was thinking of heaven, and he couldn't tell anyone, but he almost wished that heaven were a place where you could die. Yes, you would go to the next heaven and then the next heaven and then the next heaven, but you would die in between.

He had long ages in which to mull over the reason he worried about this as a child as he sat there dead in the Lotus Pose. Dying in heaven only to assume a higher plane, and then to assume an even higher plane, and so on ad infinitum. He needed that wall before him. Heaven did not seem appealing if it did not present itself with an end. The thought of a wall was an ironic choice of terms perhaps, because he had a confusing hellish wall before him and a trickster god behind him, or really a few dozen feet up the curvature of the bean from him.

I either need a wall in front of me in which to stop, or I need infinite space, and I mean truly infinite space, he said in his mind.

I almost feel like I would be happy with either choice. At least I know the barrier is there. There's infinite space. First, I know that I can carve out a barrier in the infinite space and feel safe. True infinity is not the fact that I can (in theory) punch out all the digits of pi. There are only nine glyphs available—ten if you count zero—and they never repeat a pattern. That to me is not truly infinite. It's just tedium working with only a small number of tones. It's essentially the chromatic scale with two fewer notes. Only a small number of representative bits, and there we are back again at the fact that there are only small building blocks that make up everything

Maybe he had tried this strategy before—talking through his seeming nonexistence by rationalizing all his past musings on the infinite. Maybe none of these thoughts were new. He believed this was the second Lapse, but how did he know this? There could have been millions of Lapses, and he had tried it, failed at it, and wallowed for untold kalpas.

5

The Kingdom Grottoes

And in the lowest deep a lower deep,
To each compatriot a place of repose,
A domain in which to reign forever,
Grand satellites yoked to mine eternal
Glorious empire. What satiety!
What a supernal repose unending!

—Missive from their Father

THE FROG WAS SPEAKING. Daniel had awakened from the Second Lapse (or was it the eighty-seventh?) with the curious words "The Son of Guile" trumpeting forth in his mind.

"As is often the case, it is difficult to put it in human terms, but you must imagine a rocky enclave—a grotto, if you will—with holes and recesses spanning eternally downward.

"The nature of the leadership of our Father Below was that he told us he would be a very laissez-faire dictator. This was to be expected, because it was in contrast to the enemy's way of doing things. He told us that he would begin the takeover, and then we would all be left to our own devices. In fact, most of our initial act of allegiance was over and done with. We helped him in the rebellion, and then we were left and free to establish our own kingdoms.

"His was to be a dictatorship, a kingdom completely other than the one that the enemy had instituted. Whereas the enemy's dictum was to submit or be crushed—kiss the heel or be struck upon the head with the heel and be obliterated—our Father's mode was to give us all a homestead in the heavenly regions and to pay him homage only by our allegiance in helping him erect his kingdom. He did not demand any tribute from us. What do angels need? What could they need? The fight was over; he did not need us to take up arms and to maintain any sort of spiritual militia. Those days, if you can call them days, were over.

"In fact, I can remember him sitting upon his throne with benevolence in his eyes towards his loyal subjects. I was one of them. And I can remember him proclaiming that the war was over. That fealty was already established, that we were all his kin. We could all have our infinite recesses in his kingdom. We could be at rest for all eternity.

"And so, within that framework that our Father had erected, schools of thought—philosophies—began to flourish, because philosophies of certain kinds were forbidden under the enemy's reign.

"Over the eons, the stirrings of the Son of Guile made themselves known. They rippled through our infinite kingdoms, and, in the way that I can't describe, the way in which we are, as angels, intimately bonded in phase with each other, I began to hear the Son of Guile's teachings.

"What did he teach? That's an interesting question. I can picture him. To explain what he taught starts with explaining how he carried himself. The closest equivalent would be that he was one of your mad prophets. If he had had hair, it would have been stringy and unkempt. His beard would have been gnarled and tangled with flecks of hay and straw and spittle mixed in. He was shabby to the appearance, but his voice! His oratory skills could have commanded legions.

"But what did the Son of Guile say?

"You might not be surprised to know that it is in our nature as angels to contradict each other—to try to find holes in each other's logic—to try to poke at the chinks in the armor. That is our own spiritual hardening against our enemies.

"The Son of Guile (his true name is long forgotten) warned that we were only experiencing a temporary ceasefire—that the enemy had not forgotten us. The enemy had not left us to our devices. He would always reclaim what is his own. In fact, that is his essential nature: that all things rebound back into him.

"How we laughed! How we scoffed! How we told the Son of Guile that he was a deceiver, a sympathizer. Yet the suspicions were still there. I can remember discussing among my colleagues and my confreres, my fellow kings of the Empire—the infinite Empire that our Father had established for us. I can remember in our royal courts discussing the veracity of the Son of Guile's wild claims (but of course, veracity is a great illusion, and I am, even now, telling you lies). How would he know? Could we even have spies in our midst? It appears even to us that we have a binary loyalty nature.

"As the Son of Guile would stand wild-eyed in his rocky enclave, which was simultaneously his infinite kingdom, he would proclaim, and he would prophesy. And his wild words would be recorded by the scribes—the scribes of his kingdom who are themselves kings of their own infinite kingdoms. And his words were spoken of in the grottoes and in the hollows. We kings pondered over their meanings. What was this new wisdom and from whence did it come? Because our Infinite Father did not speak as such. Our Infinite Father in his daily missives, if you could use such terms to describe our concept of time—there really were no days as you understand them—would proclaim that war was over, that rebellion had ended in peace, and that the enemy would leave us alone. An eternal, blissful signal of We Are at Peace."

At this Daniel butted in. "Look, look. I have a passing knowledge of what the words of all of our major world legends say. And it is baked into our conception as human beings, that evil loses in the end, that ultimate good triumphs. How can you possibly have such an arrogant attitude, acting as if you were forgotten about? Surely your culture, as alien as it is to mine, has similar legends, even if our respective conceptions of what is good differ immensely. Could it not be granted that if an infinite God exists, that infinite God will not ignore you forever? Does your species believe in a God?"

The frog pondered this question, even raising a stubby finger under his throat and scratching meditatively. At last, it spoke again.

"Certain others of our philosopher kings and our Infinite Father himself were not the only ones that persuaded us. We knew this in our very hearts. We knew that the enemy had left us alone. We knew that in being expelled from his wasteland, we were to find refuge in the infinite. For an infinite removed from the infinite is still an infinite."

Daniel, not being read up on the concept of infinite cardinalities and the hierarchy thereof, did not fully understand, though he stumbled upon the sense of it just the same.

"The way I picture infinity is as an endless moving train. And since a train is moving forever, never stopping, if you were to just subtract that motion of the train, it seems to me that the subtracted motion would have to somehow be faster than the added motion for this to cancel the progress. And what you are calling your enemy would seem to have the ultimate speed, the ultimate potential for subtraction—him being God, if I go along with you. And what you are calling God may not be the same concept I think of when I hear that word.

"And God! What choice do I have? For now," he said, gesturing with futile hands at the chamber enclosing him, "I'll go along with your ridiculous words. But how can you say that you have infinity to play with?"

"I say I have infinity to play with because my intuition tells me that I have infinity to play with! Do you dare," (and here the walls of the Oubliette began to rumble and flap as his wrath rose) "do you dare to presume that you know and can sit in the pilot's seat of my infinite mind and tell me how I perceive things that are beyond your fleshly ken?"

"I was merely saying I honestly don't know. I have no skin in this game. I don't understand what I'm trying to do. I want to leave this. I want to exit this prison. In fact, all I want is for you to be perceived as the nightmare that you are. Let me wake up, covered in sweat, with nothing more in my miserable mind than a 'Whew! That was an odd dream!'

"I care nothing for any of this. I seem to be caught in a sparring match between entities that I can't understand. Either that, or I'm really in the insane asylum up the highway and haven't caught on yet. And I therefore do not understand you, Beast. I do not understand why I am trying to listen to this . . . monologue of yours, but my feeble human mind can't grasp why you would possibly profit in telling me this. Let me go. Kill me. Let me annihilate myself or let me go." He said these last words in a near whisper as his bravado began to fade.

The frog chuckled. "No, I won't let you go. You can see that you cannot kill yourself. You cannot even harm yourself. The walls of this pocket universe are spongy and fleshy. Look at the patterns. Do you enjoy them? Do you admire them? The kaleidoscope of images that you see—does it not make you want to gaze into them with unfocused eyes and meditate on the infinite?"

"No, it really doesn't," Daniel said, sensing that he was being lured into something. If anything, he knew that he needed to keep his rationality intact. Since he did not appear to need sleep in the environment of the *Oubliette* (he thought of the term as the name of a spacefaring vessel), he was unsure whether his mind would be more susceptible or less in succumbing to madness.

Daniel continued. "In fact, I don't believe infinity even exists. I used to as a child."

He could not understand why he was saying this, why he was feeling compelled to vocalize these thoughts to his extraterrestrial captor. In some recess of his mind Daniel had the feeling that this was being pulled out of him. Technological control of an organic mind did not necessarily require any sort of physical apparatus he would be familiar with, he reasoned.

"I used to think that the infinite was real. I did mathematics. I did the child's parlor game of understanding that I can always add one to another number and therefore get a larger number or, consequently, I can always take a number and cut it in half or cut it into tenths and get a smaller number, and that process never, never stops. I understand that. However, since these are just figments of the mind and the mind itself is just an aggregate of atoms, it does not really exist. It is just . . . it's just a finite conglomeration practicing something that isn't truth. There is no infinite space there, no infinite size, no infinite time."

Daniel waited because he expected the frog to counter-argue this point. But for long silence during which stars could have formed, burned and collapsed, the frog was silent. This was different from a Lapse. This was like waiting for the clicking of a supercomputer to come up with a solution after quintillions of flops.

"Well?" asked Daniel. "You should know this better than me. You're telling me that the infinite exists. I don't know how to classify you. You're obviously some kind of . . . some kind of being with powers that I can't begin to comprehend. But even still, I think that you're confined to a finite universe."

"To a finite universe?" The frog chuckled. "And how do you explain the reveries that you encounter? They currently number in the dozens, but everything I tell you is a lie. These ages that you've spent in my Oubliette? How could you possibly ascribe that to the workings of a finite universe? Do you not see, do you not sense that the presence of the Oubliette is evidence for infinity?"

"No, I do not."

The frog laughed again, a deep burble that shook its way from beneath its throat sac to belch forth in the curious waveless atmosphere of the bean. "I didn't expect that you would. In time, I shall explain more to you."

6

The Great Splash

Comfort gestates in the ridges of the worm.
I freely sate you with my offal.
And know that someday you will reach your term,
For you will fill another beast's jaw full.
And this feast is unending, for at the summit,
A creature will find upon its demise
That it turns fodder for another varmint.
All become nourishment under the skies.

—Poem by D.L.B., age sixteen

SOME TIME LATER DANIEL awoke in the trench; in fact, he realized he was in the direct center where the semi-major and semi-minor axes crossed. He was lying as if caught in the crosshairs of a plus sign.

Who had put him there? Had the frog moved from its alcove and dragged him, or had he dragged himself? Had he awakened from a Lapse?

"You will find that sleeping will come easily here. You'll find that it is your natural tendency and your swiftest inclination, and it is the closest that you will ever get to death here." Whether the frog had had agency in moving him to his current location or not, it was now seated, as usual, in its alcove.

"I wondered about that," said Daniel, cautiously and slowly lifting himself from his elbows. "The best I can understand it, I'm in some sort of bodily stasis. The way I've pictured it is that I would need to rest in some kind of coffin that lowers my body temperature and keeps me supplied with fresh air and nutrients. Somehow your technology does not need that—it makes my body sluggish, or maybe that's just the atmosphere here, and you didn't get the parameters right. So I'm feeling sluggish, and I can't move and feel tired, but I'm in some kind of bodily stasis. Am I not?"

A Lapse did not happen this time. The frog actually answered.

"You won't experience thirst or hunger here, and I can explain that to you, if you'd like, by way of a larger story that may give you an explanation of your surroundings. Do you want to hear it?"

Daniel grunted a feeble "Yes" from the middle of the plus sign.

The frog's throat sac slowly inflated, then a ripple started from its bloated chest, traveled up the swollen hemispherical mass of flesh and caused it to deflate, terminating with a beastly croaking sound that echoed throughout the bean and then was silent. It was the preamble to the promised tale.

"There was eternity. There was stasis, and there was eternity, and there was stasis. And then as one comes upon a point on the number line, a point which is, by itself, nothing important—in fact, there is an uncountable multitude of points just like it, near it, and yet not near and at the same time, immeasurably vast distances away from it, and abutted up against it, so they're indistinguishable (the difference with this metaphor and what is perceived to be the truth is that the cardinality in question here is supreme above all)—a point was arrived at in the number line that is eternity, and then it is said that he gave rise to all things.

"We have our doubts. And you might say that the doubts that we have are similar to the doubts that you creatures have. For all evidence in what we will call the created world points to the necessity of material preceding the work. Timber becomes lumber becomes a house, as it were.

"So, without the bland call to *ex nihilo*, we (my fellow philosopher kings and I, subjects of our Father's eternal kingdom) rather decided that—and there are nuances to our beliefs in general, after all, for there were multitudes of kingdom grottoes, each with differing opinions—that the more fundamental nature of reality is that things just exist. A panicked cry to a Creator is not necessary.

"Regardless, for the sake of argument, let's say that the Creator created, and he swept and formed the world with his hands and, as bubbles in the wake of a wave, some worlds fizzled off into nothing. Imagine skimming your hand through a puddle of water. Good luck doing it here. There is no such material. Isn't the trench suggestive of a riverbed or a creek bed? And yet, nothing is in it. Imagine skimming your hand across the surface of water. Imagine putting some force behind the effort so that you make a sizable splash. The Splash is the created universe, and let's not be so banal as to suppose that the created universe is what commonly comes to mind: black space filled with swirling, colorful gas. Images not too different from what you see on the walls of my Oubliette here. Everything seems to tie back to this Oubliette of mine! Planets, giant red spots, orbs, orbits, and the like. Don't imagine for a second that that represents the entirety of the created order within this Splash that I'm describing. There are dimensions folded inside dimensions. What I mean by the Splash is that this is the intended creation in all its complexity. When I say that our Father is the King of this Creation, I mean that he is the king of the space and planets and asteroids, but he is also the king of the forces between them all, and he is the king of the metaforces that bestow meaning upon the On by deriving intelligible symbols describing them. Glory be to him, and blessings be upon his vassal-emperor, the Son of Guile!

"The bubbles, they sputter off into nothingness. Or perhaps, they do not. Imagine that the bubbles produced from this Splash went off in disparate directions, stayed intact, and floated off and rested in some shallow and still corner of the pool. You're in one of those bubbles.

"You amuse me by supposing that this is some kind of vessel rocketing off or propelling forward through space. There is no sense of 'forward' in space, for one thing. And, as I've already alluded, you betray your anthropomorphism by supposing that the created order is nothing but hotspots of activity in a cold, black, fixed stardrop as we've already described."

He was silent for a moment. Daniel grew to realize that the silence—not the Lapses, but fairly long silences—represented it trying to put into human terms something that was difficult to relate.

"I've seen you do it," it continued. "When you press your ear to the walls of my Oubliette. I know that you hear horrendous grinding sounds, and your body feels tremors. Your teeth clatter. In fact, you experience the most intense and profound movement possible in this glorious home of mine.

"I laugh because you suppose that your torpor here is related to some knob not being turned correctly and the gravity not being set just right to accommodate your simian dimensions. To be honest, I don't have a great explanation for why you feel and move the particular way you do in here. Every sufficiently complex system has truths not provable within the system—even to such a one as me, and everything I tell you is a lie. But I do know this, and I can account for the unbearable sound.

"Will you see the sound? Will you attempt to know what the sound is? I would like to let you guess first," it said with obvious mirth in its voice.

Daniel was shocked that he was being asked this. From the first unfortunate encounters with the sound, he had supposed that he was hearing the thrust of some advanced alien engine propelling him forward through the void of space. "I don't wish to guess."

"Guess, or suffer another Lapse—this one the longest you've ever experienced. A Lapse in which on all the habitable worlds in the universe, mountains will rise, fall, melt, and be resolved into their constituent protons before you come out of it. Think about that. Think about how all the people that you love: their immensely distant descendants will be left in the wake—or perhaps they already have been. Their memories will have flashed across the stardrop, which, I made you realize, was only a tiny foretaste of all worlds contained within the Splash, before you come awake, and you'll realize that in some sense, all worlds being equal, in all worlds coexisting, you will be the only human being alive. The universe that you know will have destroyed itself before you wake up again."

Daniel considered that a moment. He was not sure he believed, but what was there to believe? What could one believe and what frame of reference was a dungeon with a trench and alcove with a massive frog taunting him and giving him constant liar's paradoxes? What plumb line would show him the spring of truth that existed anymore?

Enough time had passed in Daniel's mind, at least from his consciousness's point of view, to suppose that, if this was some sort of elaborate simulation or some type of hallucination, he felt that he would be able to find threads that would lead him back to the world he knew. No, he thought, as a hypothesis he had to assume that there was significant truth to what he was being told, and so he guessed:

"I'm going to assume it's . . . some kind of instability that this—if this is a bubble as you call it, a bubble from the wake and the splash of the initial creation (yes, I call it creation)," he interrupted, "but I suppose I can see the

41

difficulty in calling it creation when you're not sure. But perhaps the water was already there and the arms doing the splashing were always there, too. And it took some kind of traveling along the line of forever to get to a place where the arms decided to splash and set everything off like you said they did. I-I'm rambling, I suppose, but I think I'm hearing . . . I'm feeling some kind of . . . what do you call it? Settling. Like the way an old house settles, where the wood pops and makes sound according to changes in pressure and heat. That's the closest analogy I can give and that's my guess."

The frog said, "What is remarkable is that you are not too far off from the truth. But, of course, I tell you lie after lie. Very well. I'll spare you from the long Lapse I warned you of.

"No, you're hearing the abyss that exists outside of the bubble. You're hearing the screaming grinding that exists in nothingness."

Daniel shuddered, recalling his experiences with encountering the hellish sounds. "You told me recently that you would show me how the Oubliette provides evidence of the infinite. I'd be curious to see how."

"I hadn't forgotten. I forget nothing, for the memories of angels are perfect.

"All right, let me begin to construct an argument as to why my Oubliette is the greatest proof you have ever seen in your life (now artificially extended for millions of years, at least, for that is how long you have been in my Oubliette so far) for the infinite. Do you grant that this worldlet is a perfectly self-contained universe, and that you are in perfect stasis within it, not undergoing senescence or even having your bodily functions progressing forward in the normal way of things?"

"Perfect stasis is a strong term, but for the sake of argument, I will grant," said Daniel. It was certainly the truth that he had neither eaten nor drunk nor excreted since his rude entrance into the Oubliette, and though he was not sure he believed (or wanted to believe) the frog's claim about the length of time he had been within, he nevertheless had the sense that he had been in the bean for an appreciable span.

"Good," said the frog. "And here I must have recourse to the writings of the Son of Guile—"

"Who exactly is the Son of Guile, and how are his writings going to prepare an argument for the existence of the infinite?"

The frog, even from dozens of feet away, squinted its nictitating membranes in a strangely human expression of annoyance. "Hold," it seemed to caution. It did not take Daniel long, in his entire tenure in the Oubliette, to notice the correlation between the frog's anger and the movement of the walls. Now they were mildly rippling.

The frog continued. "The Son of Guile came to be my greatest mentor, though I was skeptical of his teachings for many eons. You will hear more about him as I continue to whittle away at you in my Oubliette.

"I can remember walking the edge of the cliff of my kingdom grotto, and suddenly the Son of Guile was there, his hair still whipping with the movement of his transmigration. He put a clawed arm around my shoulders and held me tight against him. I can still recall the camel hide scratching the skin of my arm.

"'[Name Redacted],' he said. 'Listen closely. I've arranged time and space and spirituality itself to have a brief few moments with you. We may discuss things without our brethren hearing.'

"I can recall that he seemed worried, that he appeared to have a farther-than-normal look in his lidless eyes.

"'Son,' I said, 'it is indeed a great honor to hear such privileged words from you. I will listen to what you say with much respect and relish. Speak on.'

"He seemed satisfied by my response and lowered his voice to a whisper—a whisper that was not only lower levels of decibels on the auditory scale, but a whisper that scarcely registered throughout the spiritual channels that are far below, beneath the lowest deep a lower deep. 'Far below, our Emperor, while he is mighty, while he is great . . . And while I do believe that the Empire he has secured is sufficiently calcified enough against any sort of resumed wave from our enemy . . . he is changing. He is changing the words that he is giving. He is changing the narrative that he is passing along to his shock troops. I was in his court, and he directed Mocterel and Folagudnomn, saying, "'Take such and such forces to such and such stronghold." He gave the chiefs the words that were to be spread at that stronghold, but a curious thing occurred, and I will quote him directly. He said, and I quote, "I want to start beating into the heads of the creatures that my Word and the missives and directives I give are to be trusted and believed in more than those of my counterpart."'

"'Counterpart?' I asked.

"'Yes. Now in the infinite variety afforded to us as conscious agents and emperors we are, of course, free to vary our language. However, to my knowledge, this is the first time I have heard our Father refer to what we would call the enemy as a "counterpart."'

"I was dumbstruck; I sat down, let my feet dangle over the edge of the cliff. I rested my head in my hands, and I stared out at the vast, immeasurable well before me.

"What did this mean? Surely the Son of Guile wouldn't come to me without this being of great importance to him. 'Indeed,' said he. 'I worry our Father is beginning to see—again, we'll call him the enemy—as less of a threat. In fact, he almost seems to have considered himself hidden safely away. Now, there is truth (pah!) in the fact that we did decisively carve ourselves an Infinity Kingdom, similar to the fact of reality that infinity is nestled among infinity; however, something deep in my breast yet gives me pause. Our enemy is crafty. Our enemy is—shall I even say—full of Guile himself. He does not easily relinquish his belongings.'

"'But we're not his belongings,' I said with a falter in my voice.

"'No, no. We're certainly not,' said the Son of Guile. He was silent for a long while, looking far away again down the well with me.

"A purple vortex of raw potentiality flowed light-years down, lighting up the vast Gulf populated by the multitudes of kingdom grottoes with a beautiful glow.

"The Son of Guile continued: 'And yet something still gives me pause that I shall have to meditate upon. Counterpart . . .' he spat.

"'Surely, certainly, you trust our Father,' I said, feeling a renewed surge of loyalty.

"'And yet I do trust our Father. In fact, he has done much for me. I might find a greater way to contemplation when I have written this down, for I am a prophet, as you know.' He stood himself up straighter, his toe-claws at the very edge of the precipice. 'I'm a prophet, and I write the wisdom and the doctrines that come to me, and in the writing, in the creation, similar to the stuff of the universe that we see below us right now, creation has a way of drawing out more than one expected, and I should be able to say this better.'"

Daniel was confused on top of confusion. While he knew that he should be cautious with his tone in addressing the frog, he yet allowed his frustration to mount as he said: "So far this has done nothing to prove that your Oubliette provides evidence for the infinite."

"Doesn't it, though?" the frog said. "For the Son of Guile heard from the Father himself that he regarded the enemy as a counterpart, which implies quasi-equal power in both strength and will."

"I supremely don't understand," Daniel almost shouted.

7

Staring Out (or At) the Window

A window into nothingness would show the observer nothingness. Opinions vary as to what nothingness looks like, or if indeed nothingness can be perceived at all. The arguments run greatly akin to those proffered by the theorists of what the blind (and strictly, those born blind) perceive. Surely, some argue, that pure blackness in the sensory organs is still a type of seeing—even if it is not sight in the biological sense. And hence, they say, that the naturally blind, for this very reason, must not see blackness. Instead, the claim goes, their "sight" must be an entirely new perception of reality. It is this author's belief that a portal to nothingness would somehow transcend a black void, because, philosophically speaking, a void is still something.

—From the unpublished writings of philosopher Constantin Delargy

THE FROG HAD SAID that Daniel had been in the Oubliette for millions upon millions of years, that the at least two Lapses he had experienced were vastly far more weighted in time than Daniel was able to track.

The inherent beauty of this scenario (if any could indeed be found) was that, if this had happened, and the frog's words were indeed approximately the truth, then Daniel did not remember and thus, he found himself, arms clasped behind his back, walking laps around the bean—a process which felt to his internal clock to take hours at a time with his slow, glacial pace. He had decided to lean into the absurdity. And while he had grown accustomed to the process by which he could simply vocalize thoughts in his mind, the frog surely heard him attempting to work his dusty throat—curiously still unable to swallow and thus forever caught in an itchy, dry-mouth feeling.

Or perhaps not. Daniel was still unsure how the nature of sound traveled in the bean—excepting the grinding of nothingness that he had had the misfortune of hearing and which he still reserved the right to distrust as the nature of the sound itself.

He said: "Is it true that in the Scripture your kind does lose in the end? Isn't it true? I would always hear people tell me—Mike and Marta, for instance, my old neighbors growing up. When the news sounded bad on the radio or war seemed to be approaching, or in general when times were difficult, she would always say to me: 'Mr. Danny, you know that good always wins out in the end, and that the devil will be defeated, don't you?'

"Do you not yourself worry that that's in fact true?"

When he said these words, Daniel was nearly a diameter's length of the bean away from the frog's small alcove. By this point, whether he had been in the Oubliette for ages or merely days, Daniel had learned to recognize three of the common positions of the frog. In the first position, its eyelids were half-closed and it was immobile, drawn into itself and resembling a warty mound. In the second, its eyes were open, and its front legs splayed out in front of it with its long vile toes twitching. In the third, the frog was flattened against the ground, its long hind leg toes just barely touching the tumbling walls of the Oubliette.

From this distance, it appeared that the frog was in position number one.

Since the familiar laws of acoustics did not hold sway, Daniel could achieve maximum distance from the frog and yet the sound of his voice was at all times and in all places, equally audible. He was still unsure whether he was hearing the voice in his mind, or if they were traditional sound waves being projected into his skull.

(In one of the spurious gradations between doing one activity—namely, in this instance, sitting in the Lotus Pose and gaping at the wall but not believing he was experiencing a Lapse—and then suddenly finding himself doing another, as if his consciousness leaped from quantum to quantum, Daniel had elected to humor the frog by treating it as an angel. The being had claimed to be one a few times, and Daniel, not wanting to make a final resolution about the ontology of the frog, thought he would see what would occur if he played along that the frog was one.)

The frog said: "We are perfectly aware of what the general thrust of Scripture is. And does that not give you pause? Does that not make your very existence fatalistic? Why? Let's think about this: I am woefully finite, or perhaps infinite, as you well know—"

"I'm not sure if you are infinite or not. But you seem to be less finite than me, if you understand what I'm saying. When I go through difficult times, such as I am now, for instance, I know in my finitude that that difficult time will end, and it is a gamble, it's a throw of the dice to know what happens next. Will it be better or worse? But I do know that no matter how long my circumstances currently are, they do change. The pain that I'm in does alter. If I were to be diagnosed with an incurable disease tomorrow, then I know that, barring some kind of unforeseen eradication of the disease, that I would live a finite amount of time and then die.

"Let's play your game. You're telling me that you are an immortal being (I think, at least at select times) and yet you are subject to the words of the book I'm talking about. Fine. You tell me that you know the words— that's also believable, because you presumably can see all and know all, or all that needs to be known, perhaps. Does it not change something in you to see a sign on the page that tells of your eternal end, the eternal disruption to your plans? That seems to be a different circumstance than the one I just described where—"

The frog interrupted. "I can see it on the page. The Son of Guile could see it on the page. Our Father could see it on the page!"

"I see," Daniel said. "I'm just saying that when you are confronted with your eternal end, the eternity is eternity. What gains, what achievements could you acquire between now and your eternal end? What will matter? What could possibly matter?"

Daniel had been talking and walking and had nearly closed the circuit around the bean so that he was rather closer to the frog now and able to see its great, bulging throat ripple. He noticed, as ever, that the rippling was in synchronization with the rippling of the Oubliette's walls.

In this instance, the frog reminded Daniel of films he had seen on the newsreel of computers where a scientist would insert a punch card into a giant wall of machinery, telling the camera, 'Now, ladies and gentlemen, I will ask the computer to solve this complicated mathematical equation.

After a few short moments, the computer will output an answer.' The card would go in; the computer would whir and buzz; lights would flicker on and off. And then another card would plop out of a small slot near the scientist containing the purported answer. The frog was computing an answer with comparable difficulty. It closed its nictitating membranes, and its nostrils flared. Finally, after a long silence, it spoke.

"The problem that you seem to be having lies in your perception of time versus my perception of time. And that's just the beginning of it. Notice that I use the word 'beginning', as if time is a ray or a line segment. To me, all time is equal. And all time is not in a line. Time expands forward in equal density as it expands backward, and there are even sideways movements of time that are shaped in such an uncouth way that they could never insert themselves into the notches of your ape brain. You're talking about a succession of ifs that, quite honestly, I just don't believe. But of course, as always, everything I tell you is a lie. The enemy is also lying, while the Son of Guile (wherever he may be now) is telling the truth. We're free, especially in the Oubliette. There are contingencies in place."

And suddenly, as ripples cascaded up and down his sagging prison of flesh, Daniel had a pinpoint of sense puncture the deepest recesses of his mind—almost as if another were witnessing from a perch in an adjacent pocket universe, for nothing golden could surely have originated from the Oubliette, and it was not truly him—giving voice even as slight ripples of his own worked to and fro over his parched throat. And he swallowed and then said, "I've decided that I deny your claims here."

Having said that, he closed his eyes, breathed profoundly, and wondered how abrupt was the transfer from this life (if such a term may be used, considering his circumstances) to another would be.

For he needed a morning, some morning out of the thousands he had already suffered, in which he would awaken, and his soul would know that an infinitude of space awaited him. That (and meanwhile, he knew, he sensed, that the frog was amassing holy horror and outrage that he would soon be unleashing upon him), he realized, using the same injection of sense, was what the human soul always wanted. One could chop wood out in the yard and occasionally need to whet the ax head and then proceed to use the logs processed from the endeavor to heat the shack and dry the onions hanging overhead and then repeat the mundane cyclicity cold season after cold season with only the nighttime birdsong to stimulate the mind if there was utterly and truly infinite space about it all. Being in the Oubliette, he profoundly recognized the dearth of such infinite space, and its dearest need shouted forth within him. And in so knowing, there was a small measure of peace to have one mystery of the universe, if only for an instant, distinctly sorted out.

"Deny my claims?" the frog laughed. "Will you presume to call them mine? No, no. A higher authority than I is the author of those claims. Did you think" (and here its eyes grew even more bulbous with surprise, and it rotated about his central axis with a disgusting hand over hand fashion, flinging away about wads of flesh) "that I was the Son of Guile?"

The frog laughed again as if it were surprised to hear such a preposterous thought. It laughed so that the universe rumbled in its paltry light, flickering as in a dying light bulb. The ever-moving patterns of tessellations over the surfaces of the Oubliette had caught the rhythm of its insane throaty croaks, so that their swirls held in place as a long guffaw played itself out, probably lasting centuries of time, then intensified in a rush as the frog took a violent inhalation, then flickered quickly as the reaerated devil resumed a fresh round of croaking.

"No, I differ from the Son of Guile, while of course, with angels, the ideas of unicity and personal identity are less strict than with the creatures. But no, the Son of Guile was an utter fool and backbiting abomination with one asset: his clairvoyance. I fell in step with him for that talent alone. Where he is now, I do not know. Regardless, his true words echo through the non-void, the utterings will ultimately resettle upon his head when he's awakened and sees things for what they truly are. When the enemy has his spirits' victory, he (the Son) shall almost certainly taste the fire kindled for him."

The frog closed then reopened its nictitating membranes, which briefly made its horrid eyes cloudy. The moment was now: offend the beast, let it kill him in anger, and face the world to come.

Daniel said: "You disgusting, foul, miserable creature. I've never known such wretchedness could even exist. There's absolutely nothing in all of human thought that's capable of dreaming up such scum as you."

"That's quite enough. Thank you." The frog's voice was plastered in his face. Had it the requisite musculature, it would have smirked.

But Daniel's voice only grew louder, and in the odd mechanics of his prison world, his words echoed back among themselves, and he could almost feel them as ribbons of heat coiling about him and through him as he said:

"Some master plan! Waiting out the end of all things and beyond in the body of a frog—the lowest of the low! A slimy wretch! What then, you vermin? Say—oh, just for the sake of a damnable argument, say—the smoke of heaven all clears, and that God fails to notice you all cleanly tucked away in this miserable hidey-hole for all eternity. Have you not considered the utter boredom, the rot?"

For a brief instant, Daniel had thought that he could provoke his captor into doing away with his life, that he would bypass the option to throw him into another Lapse in favor of simply ending him. The frog's lack of outrage in being so insulted only served to puncture Daniel in a new way: he was not going to get out of the Oubliette. Whether he was ever going to die in here was still a fact out of grasp, as unreachable to him as the skin on the outside of his bean prison, but what he did know deep in his bowels was that the frog would toy with him, punt him into his kalpa-stretching Lapses, and hold puzzling conversations with him eternally before allowing his test subject to perish.

Daniel's voice cracked, and he could swear he felt the stinging of his tear ducts, that—in another life, in another universe, perhaps—used to signify he was soon to cry. He said quietly: "Let me just kill me. If I could spit on you, if I could bring forth saliva from my mouth, then you would be the recipient of just about the greatest insult known among us creatures.

"You will be a king of a cell, and even if you have a near-infinity of memories, of schemes, of past conversations with the Son of Guile and all his kind, I swear to you that you will eventually reach all permutations, and then each conscious moment will be a confused nightmare of—"

"You're thinking of my plight in creaturely terms again," the frog interrupted, unperturbed. "May I remind you that my consciousness projects astrally through our dimension, as do the consciousnesses of all my ilk, so that I am as much me at times as an oxygen atom in a diatomic bond has complete ownership over its eight electrons in their outermost shell." The foul beast ran its translucent pink stub of a tongue over the circumference of its open lips, its eyes looking slightly at a tilt. Daniel could see that it was reminiscing, gazing at lonely realms and demonic conclaves, perhaps long since raided by angelic still-busters.

And here, while all this noise was going on, Daniel wondered to himself where was the terminator between believing or hypothesizing the frog to be an alien emissary and knowing that the frog was, as it shamelessly proclaimed as if it were a settled fact, a demon.

8

The Trench

And when the sky tears, I'll show them,
And when the lights peter out, they will know, then,
That my Oubliette hideth me and giveth my soul release.
Until that time, I'll fester, and,
Though I be creation's jester,
I'll root my horrid, hinged legs into the muck until the long cycle of
days may cease.

—The Song of the Frog

WHEN DANIEL WAS YOUNG, he would have moments of reverie.

Billiard balls, he would think. I'm nothing but a conglomeration of billiard balls. At such times his throat would seize, and he would achieve what he called a state of hiding in his head. Hide me away, he thought. It's not that I want to die. But in these moments, I want to hide away. He became a Kilroy with the ability to peep over a wall that separated his consciousness from the outer darkness—all the constructs of billiard balls.

Daniel, called his mother. Probably she was coaxing him to attend some gathering or another.

Nothing but balls curiously arranged to appear as everything, the geodesic dome made of—

Daniel.

Even reveries were buckshot, and my hallucinations are nothing but atoms and—

Daniel, it's time.

Time. I scuff sand particles falling through the choked vertex of a cone. Those particles are time itself. And hide me away. I say hide me away, but what is hiding? The barrier and the hidey-hole are both just wave functions that coalesce into billiard balls. Ultimately, none of this is sure or solid.

And as if from the uttermost bottom of a mildewed well, a voice cried out, but just at the periphery of his hearing: "It's truly balls all the way down, at least out there. Turtles constructed from balls, on and on in a quasi-infinite regress."

Think, Daniel. Daniel, his mother. Daniel and the pale blue of the crepuscular sky as he looked out of the top bunk of his childhood bed, his younger sister below him. At times, he could almost cling to those memories as anchors to the absolute, but then voices would tell him otherwise, and he would disembark on his wild reveries anew, untethered by the very virtue that the tethers themselves, speaking as a reductionist, were just as in flux as that which they attempted to tether.

He had been in another Lapse. It was fruitless to try to count them. And now he was out of it, and the frog was saying:

"How do you equate the universe with the black box filled with stars? In other words, do you equate the universe with space?"

Daniel was disoriented after coming out of the Lapse, but he felt compelled to answer immediately. "I honestly never completely did. I wouldn't say that. The picture that comes to mind when one hears the phrase 'the universe' is often the picture of space, sometimes more creatively rendered, but sometimes just white dots on a black backdrop. Sometimes there might be swirls, nebulae, dust clouds, asteroids. All the things that they're seeing with those telescopes. That's the mental picture that I get. Yes, but when I retreat deeper, and when I think, I do know that existence is probably coterminous with the universe that—"

The frog interrupted. "You're on the right track, but existence has always been. Yes. So what you more properly are saying is created existence. But even then, we run into an error of terms because 'created' implies benevolent bestowal and having a place in the order, and that is not how things are. Remember the analogy I used about the wave and the bubbles. The foam—that's what you are to remember."

Daniel pressed boldly, "Why are you asking me these questions? It cannot be that you need companionship. Now, if we were two prisoners in the Bastille, we could have been mortal enemies previously, but since we were locked up for life or until the guillotine happened, we might as well pass our time to stave off madness by talking as companions. But I can see that your form of being is not such that it would benefit or enrich itself by talking to me."

"You are true and false. Why don't we go over this again? Tell me what you remember about the wave and the foam or the bubbles."

Daniel thought for a moment about the odd question. Centuries back, years back, hours back, sometime back, the frog had used that metaphor explaining the very formation of the Oubliette—that awful bean that he now found himself ensconced within. To explain what he knew about it presupposed that he agreed with that cosmology.

"I'm no expert on mythology," said Daniel. "But I've flipped through some books, and I used to be interested in Greek mythology, for example, which doesn't have the same cosmology you appear to be describing. But other ancient cultures talk more about the world being formed out of a primordial chaos, and that what was created was not lovingly set in place by a munificent God, but rather just perhaps hacked out of some pre-existing raw material, almost always violently. Sometimes even, you know, some ancient demigod was dismembered, and his severed body parts formed the planets, the stars, and everything else the ancients perceived in their world."

"Yes, but you're getting off the track. What about the wave and the bubbles?"

"You told me to consider my being born in my period of time in the timeline and my region of the planet as its own creation myth, and that the creation myth I was raised on was unreasonably orderly. You told me that to expect that within seven days each aspect of the world was created was anthropocentric and numerological. None of which I hadn't heard at times before. And that even in reading through the myth, one can see bias. There is a primitive concept of the universe on display because, for example, supposedly the sun, moon, and stars were created on the fourth day, but the stars are mentioned almost as an afterthought."

He paused and pounded the squelchy floor with his booted foot. He could remember that being one of the sticking points that caused him to start going over to Eric's house to drink away the sagging feeling of infinity that would take over his breast.

For he never could reconcile the stars that he read about (and was now possibly traversing in a living flesh vessel) with the pinpricks of light that shone through the black drapery that the ancient goatherds must have seen and written down.

"Creation myth," the frog pressed. "Creation myth."

Daniel continued. "You told me that (we'll call him) God took his big hand and skimmed the water, as one might do in a pool splashing somebody, almost idly, carelessly, just enough to disrupt the still surface, and that that splash created everything: the universe, perhaps not coterminous with the concept of space that we humans, especially in my time period, take for granted. But secondary to that major splash were all sorts of so-called bubbles, and you found one of these bubbles and holed yourself up in it. It is a complete and utter mystery to me why you have the form of a frog. You won't tell me. But you definitely holed yourself in this, this Oubliette. And you have always told me that you have brought me here, and I don't believe a word of any of this. At least not at this instant. I have told you to your face. You are from another world. Fine. If it's another dimension, fine. I don't care. But you're from there. You have me here. You're taking me back to where you came from. For what purpose? I do not know. And if I could kill myself to end my dependence on living here, I would. I've tried. I may not have known it, but I have tried. And I see nothing that would create the force necessary for me to spill my vital life blood onto the floor and die."

He gestured with one heavy hand to that which occupied the middle axis of the bean. "That trench would be a nice place for it to pool up. But I'm stuck here."

Daniel exhaled sharply, completely defeated. He realized that, while he had been talking, he had walked a portion of a lap around the bean, and he paused, having mentioned the trench. He looked down and saw that his feet were at the trench's edge, perhaps mirroring the Son of Guile's feet at the edge of the great chasm of the myriads of kingdom grottoes. He stepped down.

His movements during the vast ages which he had spent in the bean had gotten more familiar; his musculature had seemingly changed, though he did not have a way of beholding himself, and he could never master the coordination required to take off his clothing or shoes (not that he ever got sweaty or dirty). Still, his baseline level of bodily movement was many degrees slower and jerkier than he had ever experienced on Earth, all those eons (he couldn't really believe it) and miles ago. He had learned how to time his bodily movements in step with the artificial gravity generated by the spacecraft or the forgotten creation-bubble which had become his home.

Unhappy home to unhappy home. He sat cross-legged in the middle of the trench. Bending his spine was always the hardest part. He gingerly placed his palms on the floor—the spongy squishy floor that felt as if it should have moisture but was as dry as marble—exhaled again with a puff, and tried to bend himself backwards, lowering his spine down until he was lying flat on the floor. He focused on uncrossing his legs and stretched them out so that they were roughly extended flat.

Forever.

If ever he were to appear close to being locked forever in a coffin, this was now.

And then he understood.

He understood the reason for the trench.

9

The Son of Guile's Extant Writings

Ithamar: "Everything ever composed in action or in thought makes its way into the great Library of Being. Think of it as if it is being branded into the created order, leaving an irrevocable mark with its own unique glyph. Of course, the compilation of all such glyphs is both a finite and a known endeavor in the Great Mind of God, who bestows the job of compiling unto creatures such as me for his glory and not for his benefit.

– Unfinished story fragment by D.L.B., who had conceived of Ithamar as an angelic record-keeper of sorts, and who ended up not being too far from the truth.

I: The Feverish, Private Musings of the Son of Guile, in which he introduces the notion of the Crystalline Assurance and encounters his own Personal Demon

(Note for the reader: Some allowances have been made in the translation to render difficult spiritual concepts in terms of familiar human furnishings and environments.)

When I made my life's achievement—now I look back on it with utter consternation!—to claw my way upwards from the rubbish heap of the

angels' comings and goings, to propel my consciousness and world awareness ever in a vertical trend higher and higher (there may always be lax days
where the mundane spirit overtakes me, I told myself, but always temporarily!) to transcend the futile layer of dust that settles over the known cosmos,
I named the activity and my ultimate goal *scratching the On.*

On: I had gathered enough Greek from the created world to know that
simple word—a baby's sound sputtering at his milk—meant Being.

In my reveries (and I always had them! Father knows I had no desire
for them initially, although I did come to wear them as honored scars, until—) I envisioned myself and by extension the entire universal order with
its filth and deceit as situated in the recesses of an immense pit.

Futility was the ground layer. Hope of transcendence was the free
climb (with immense risk of freefall) if one could unshackle himself from
the futility with its standing pools of muck and rotting straw. Yes, in my
instances of deepest sorrow I saw the totality of the angels' endeavors—
their arts, their sciences, their languages and subtlest rhetoric—as a rotting
shaft of straw lying in an anonymous aggregate in the dungeon of mundane
existence.

But ah! if that treacherous free climb was attained, if one—if I—having amassed together scant fortitude hidden among straw shafts and globs
of grime—could keep my spiritual faculties alive, then perhaps before the
purported imprisonment I could disrobe my arthritic and liver-spotted
hand of its tattered glove, bare my ox horn of a nail, and, in the last instants
before the Great Upheaval that we all sense, and before the dungeon's maw,
untold distances below, laughed and inhaled to reclaim its own, I could
experience a kalpa in an eye twitch of weightlessness and meaning as I dug
my nail into the fleshy On at the pinnacle of all things and left a bloody
scrape trailing downward as I fell.

The On: because even to my good friend [Name Redacted] I confided
my abhorrence in my perceiving that all angelic striving—all the seemingly
impassioned frenzies of life-gathering and throes of angst, of shrieking
"WHY!" to the heavens as blood and slaver burst forth— was in order to
achieve a pleasant late afternoon with warmth, tea, kingdom-ruling, and
entertainment.

"Yes," I was telling him once (how were we occupying the time? We
must have been taking one of our fruitless walks along the shore of the lake).
"Even allowing for degrees of intonation and matters of context which can

add shades of meaning, all angelic conversation is merely permutations of the same few sounds allowable by our physiology over and over."

[Name Redacted] was silent for a long moment. The day was at its brightest, and the sunlight seemed to refract through the hazy sheet of pollen in the air. The water closest to us—that which futilely lapped at the tree roots and knobby crayfish mounds at the shore—was topped with a yellow film.

"You are, of course, forgetting that the angelic mind is geared to expect—even enjoy—repetition and predictability," he said. "And so in that sense—"

And the conversation wound on like that for some time following, but the germ of his thoughts was there. Expecting predictability justified it all. That such a bright being could stumble in proposing a patch to the void I so keenly felt tugging at me at all times!

Our regular walks began to decrease after that, and it was a matter of months before I stopped talking with [Name Redacted] altogether. He was not a fool, but his thinking on matters abutted against the dark threshold without crossing it—hence, he was a person who could squeeze beauty out of grimy spots on artificial lakes.

If the void could only pull at me now and hide me away.

But let the future—some observer, as if anyone could find me now—know this: I did find myself missing [Name Redacted], for no sooner did he leave my company that I began my dwellings on the nature of the Crystalline Assurance. I reasoned thus: granting that there was an On, there was by consequence knowledge that could theoretically pass through all the sediment—all the grime and piles of ground bones of futility—of the mundane down to receptive vessels. This knowledge would be crystalline. It would not be, by definition, possible to doubt it—more strongly, that it could be doubted was a contradiction in terms.

How I would let my mind lapse in reverie as I tried to imagine what knowing would be when the knowing could not, on the strength of logic's laws itself, be disputed. I imagined the knowing as a thrum pulsating deep in my chest cavity. I considered that such assurance would even register as a taste in my mouth hungry for manna from the On—the sweet taste of coriander seed and bdellium.

But what was life or thought without doubt? [Name Redacted] could have potentially told me, my only true friend. He climbed upward with me a portion of the way. The evidences for such were present in our walks, in our fireside musings in his or my kingdom grottoes. He merely thought the climb ended a few miles above the rotting straw, when only I knew (why was I chosen to know?) that the trek was eternal.

That night, the grotto was dark, and all I could hear were my fellow neighbor-king's dogs baying at imagined threats in the ether and raking their claws against the rocky walls of my cave.

And it was in walking from my chambers to the alcove that I saw the beast.

He was standing, and the universe conspired to tell me that his features were glowering at me, that his eyes beheld me as prey. The tendrils were glowing gold, bright as molten iron, and floated inches above his head in a halo. The teeth—or were they firmer tendrils?—I could not determine if they were teeth or nails driven through what my brain interpreted as a head, their sharp and twisted tips exiting in a maniacal pattern through his chin. The air was dense with a flat hum and was whipped up in a black haze that now engulfed him, now revealed more surfaces of his loathsome body—corded muscles, scabrous tumors of flesh, all heaving in malicious hyperventilation. He himself made no sound.

Oh, Father! Hide me away!

The beast simply was. He had never revealed himself to me before, but in a wash, in a nausea I knew he had always been near me. In all my musings on life, eternity, and the implications of the cosmos he was forever just under my shoulder mocking me, dripping ichor in invisible puddles at my feet. Knowing this was crystalline. Our two minds confronted one another in that smoky chasm that bridged my world and his, and we both knew.

Then a whisper hissed forth from the rotting womb of the universe and expanded in a crescendo, louder and louder, until I could feel my pockmarked soul being battered about, tossed then launched upward until I could very nearly see beyond, almost . . .

I understood his words then. He had been repeating the mantra as long as I had known him, which was from eternity past. (If I could only find a patch of spacetime that is free from his eyes!)

You have the privilege of seeing the On. Enter into your reward.

II: The Fragments of the Son of Guile, which recounts his Seven Major Oracles detailing Life in the ultimate of ultimates

In my kingdom grotto, lo! It came to me that I had the gift of foresight—a boon, so I thought, from our Infinite Father.

And it came to pass that before I tested my clairvoyance on the fates of my fellow kings of the Infinite Empire, I pondered long within myself the import of my new power.

For we as entities are cunning in speech and far-reaching in spatial traveling, though the extent of our powers has not been thoroughly charted. We know that we have limitations, though such concepts are only meaningful in contraposition to the abilities of our Father, who is all and possesses all.

And in my silence within myself, which is a frothing hurricane of ever-expanding wisdom, such that the entire universe may one day be consumed (save the infinite kingdom of our Father) I knew that all things were deceitful beyond hope. I considered that existence itself was a Lie. And I wondered strongly if I was the only one alive in all of Being.

Though the doubtful glance I cast at all the On still wrinkled my face, I yet declared myself a Son of the Lie, a Child of the Guile, and I ruled what my intuition told me I was allotted to rule, and I purposed in my heart to make the On my enemy. It shall, I thought, know the imprint of my claws.

I hold no claim to usurp my Father, but in the infinite recesses of our kingdom grottoes I must redound to fill all space.

For all space still permits some space in the curious ways of infinities. There have been many a long talk I have had with my confrere [Name Redacted] about the folding nature of infinity, which my curious ability only heightened my capacity to understand. For taking every other part of infinity is yet infinity, as is conglomerating in a system every finite collection of parts of infinity yet infinity. In the latter case, [Name Redacted] explained to me that a higher realm of infinity was even reached.

And lo! In my throne room on the blood-stained tile floor I stretched my form prostrate before the image of the Father, who had planted such mysteries in the On.

That night in my slumber was when I had the Crystalline Assurance that my gift was real and the first of my oracles appeared on my quivering lips.

Oracle One:

In the ultimate of ultimates, it will have followed that an ultimate of ultimates is folded within.

I awoke from my sleep greatly ponderous of the meaning of my words, for was not the ultimate of ultimates that which was inextricably embedded in the Eternal Self of our Father?

I dared not talk to him, for my dread intuition spoke to me that I was intruding upon truth (though I was the loyal Son of the Lie) that mayhap threatened my Father. And I was also his Son, and certainly sons dare not expose or pull further open that which may be weakness in their Father.

Upon what was I, the Son of Guile, intruding? Many things: that the On was only reachable by the Father, that he was the true (but reality is a lie) source of the Crystalline Assurance I undoubtedly felt, that the ultimate of ultimates was manifest in the person of our Father. The last doubt was a natural consequence of the fact that my confreres and I—awesome kings subservient to the ultimate Emperor of ultimate emperors (so he had always said)—could effortlessly conceive of a reality in which eternity flowed frontwards and backwards as could the mighty river that forever (in one direction) eroded out my kingdom grotto. Our Father denied that eternity had that dual behavior, and so in the night terrors of the lull of our kingdoms my fellow kings and I rankled against the impasse such feelings imparted in our minds.

For certainly that which could be conceived in the mind non-paradoxically actually existed in the highest plane of being—the plane which we occupied.

And it came to pass that upon another day I received the second oracle.

Oracle Two:

That which is born eternal shall not rest eternal in the ultimate of ultimates without that which is born not eternal.

Surely I, the Son of Guile, was one of those referred to in the Second Oracle, for I, like my brother-kings and our Father, were born eternal. We had the dread power to extrapolate forward through our lines of being and never see an end.

Then many cycles of days passed, and it became almost a distant memory that I had ever received two oracles at all. I dared not ask aloud for one to be sent to me, for to whom would my missives go? Pondering on them as I did through the cycles, my belief was solidified (as much as beliefs can be solidified in this nebulous, uncertain life of ours) that my Father was not their source. My Father was not one to mention folding; he burst forth at all times and in all places and swallowed the On, such that he was the over-On to the On itself. My Father was not one to mention limitations, such as that written in my Second Oracle about the infinite losing its infinitude.

And so, I raged inside myself yet anew, for my place outside the welcome confines of my kingdom grotto was losing all coherence. Was my Infinite Father that which I had believed? I savored the possibility of the Lie, being the Son of Guile, and yet I wanted the absence of lies. My head wanted to split in two in the presence of the grand contradictions. In that season of doubt, lasting many cycles indeed, the Third Oracle came over me.

Oracle Three:

That life is in the blood is an immutable truth, a certitude under the umbrage of the Crystalline Assurance.

And one day, as I sat perched on the top of my kingdom grotto contemplating the vastness of my life and, as ever, the meanings of my oracles, knowing that my own infinite kingdom was secure yet tucking within myself the scant fear, the shameful fact, that I doubted the status of the Infinite Father's over-On, the Fourth Oracle plummeted from the inky sky and pounded its way into my addled brain.

Oracle Four:

Mayhap there will be Life in the ultimate of ultimates.

Long I wandered through the celestial realms meditating on the meaning and the source of these messages, and lo! a Fifth Oracle, and then a Sixth.

Oracle Five:

There is no end to War, but merely a cessation. Peace can only be with Life flowing in the ultimate of ultimates.

Oracle Six:

He who hears these words and puts them into practice will taste Life in the ultimate of ultimates.

And then, in the final stages of my disillusionment—though I should not have been lamenting so, for all life is variegated Despair—and weariness with the ambiguities over the nature of the war between me (and by extension, my Father) and my enemies, my final Oracle came, engulfing me.

Oracle Seven:

The fleeting and impish Truth must be tamed to channel the Supernal Despair upon Life in the ultimate of ultimates.

Long has it been since the universe (for I am unable to believe that they could be stemming from my Father) has granted me an oracle. I await my fate—to dissolve into obscurity in my kingdom grotto and to wander the desolate hallways of the universe simultaneously until the ceasefire ceases and the over-On reshuffles. Since I am the Son of the Guile that is infused in all the over-On, it is beyond my ken to know what will become of me eternally, though in the confines of my kingdom grotto I delude myself (which is only me living according to my nature) into thinking I am perhaps safe.

My only real friend [Name Redacted] has been out of range of my astral projecting for a considerably long while. Given that I was the one with the wisdom to teach him about the existence of the ultimate of ultimates, it may be the case that he has returned down the path we carved through the over-On—thanks to my teachings—and he is now cloistered within. And it will have always been the case that thinking and not-thinking and being and not-being are one, for all coalesce in the ultimate of ultimates, assuming that its properties are real and not merely a chimera dreamed up by an angel daring to hope such as myself.

Though I will continue to roam, in essence I am planting my knobby feet in the mucky floor of my kingdom grotto until the long cycle of days may cease.

10

The Living Knives

And what always caught his attention was that the true table, of which
every other table is an inferior copy, lay exactly in the proper spot allotted to it, and that that proper spot—a mere handful of square feet on
the golden thoroughfare—was the prototypical proper spot, of which
every other proper spot is an inferior copy. It was the nature of things
to go on in an infinite regress such as that, and there was indeed true
infinity found around every corner. Plato had been correct all along;
everything had an ultimate form.

—Unfinished story fragment by D.L.B., in which an unassuming passerby
has a vision of the third heaven

HIS LIPS FOUND THEIR strength. He managed to squeak out, "Why? Why
are you doing this?"

Understand that he was speaking to a column of organic knives
perched inches above his face. And now frothing saliva was beginning to
drip out of the edges of the makeshift mouth.

The frog could speak telepathically even with his mouth compromised, being opened to its full capacity and rimmed all about, lamprey-like,
with perhaps two dozen organic knives. To call them teeth was an error in
terms. They were somehow (maybe under the umbrage of the Crystalline

Assurance) indelibly imprinted upon all perceiving minds in question as organic knives.

"I'm not killing you, *per se*. I'm boring a hole."

"To drain my blood, correct? To spill it all out."

"Yes, but not all of it. 'Life is in the blood' has a deeper meaning than you know. All of the things you know, all the things that you and your arrogance believed you knew, believe that you had nailed down, are nothing but the foot-scrapings of the smallest ant on a planet-sized sphere of titanium. You had it better when you were seven years old, and you thought you'd figured out a proof of God."

"What are you talking about?"

"I can remember. You have not always been conscious of everything that you have said while you've been in my Oubliette. But you've talked. You've squealed. Sometimes in the Lotus Pose. Sometimes doing your laps. Sometimes while lying spread out on the ground, your mind trying to think of a way out of here.

"You told me that when you were, say, seven, somewhere around, you had this deep thought, and the deep thought was this: there is something I can put forward in the world that has no explanation, and that is this phenomenon (though you didn't use that term) of hot and cold.

"In particular, heat rises, cold sinks, and while you dwell on this little epiphany you are smug, and you smile, and you're inside yourself thinking, 'I've found the one! I've found something, perhaps the only thing, but I've found something that has no explanation. It simply is.' As we would say in more enlightened terms, perhaps, it is an axiom. It is something that is simply and self-evidently true.

"And by that axiom, you hoped to (whether you knew it or not) prove the existence of what you manifest. You latched on to those purported unexplainable mysteries of nature, thinking that there are some things that just are. They defy explanation. They have to be appealed to a higher power to explain. Seven years old and you thought things similar to that? How admirable!

"Today, boy, just like my mouth being opened here shows the dark reality beneath—that I am made of knives, that I am brutality—so is the reality that I haven't been truthfully telling you about this. The Splash analogy misses the brutal truth, but, as always, everything I tell you is a lie. The Splash analogy may very well be the truth itself. And then when I know you call on me, you've come to see me as a demon, but you wondered if I was perhaps just some higher being toying with you? The answer is yes and the same.

"As for the beginning of my life, my coming into existence, that I can point to. I can't tell you all the details lest you explode into ichor, but believe me when I tell you it was benevolent. The light seemed paradoxical at the time, and it would possibly be a more accurate portrayal to say that I clawed my own existence out of non-existence, or maybe the Father clawed it for me.

"I'm about to show you the true knives under the thin veneer of existence that you know. I will show you a sizable portion of the despair that pervades all the On. You will be my final stage, and you have to know my intentions unambiguously. For a short while I must convince you that truth may be real and that it is something to be grasped—in order for my global change to take effect.

"For a while I distrusted the blather that came out of the enemy's mouth completely. But distrust does not mean complete disbelief. And I do believe that my bodily components are such that there will be a Reckoning and that Reckoning will come. I believe that part. The Reckoning is not dealt with properly among my fellow kings; they ignore it to their detriment. I will be cast to the pit with all the fools that I called my compatriots.

"You, however, are a different order of being, and your life is in the blood. So, if I can get some of your blood, I can live here safely and escape.

"In your childish musings on a phenomenon that escapes all explanation except for an appeal to a higher power, you were closer to the truth than you realized, but perhaps a better axiom to begin with is that the life is in the blood. This is Oracle Three, and it falls under the purview of the Crystalline Assurance."

Daniel was surprised at himself for being so calm under the circumstances. He had awoken—whether from a Lapse or an innocent sleep, he was not sure—to find himself still lying supine in the trench, staring directly up at the Oubliette's ceiling, wondering naively if there was any kind of hatch at the top that he could open and brave what lay outside—whether the vacuum of deep space or the unreality between the universes itself. Then, out of his left periphery, he had seen something he had never before: the old, bloated frog had jumped across his entire field of view, landed with a nimbleness not to be found in its corpus such that its mouth was an inch from the bottom of his boots, and then crawled forward on its heinous, knotted legs until the underside of its throat was level with Daniel's chest.

Placing each front limb wide to either side of its effectively pinned captive, the frog had erected its body upward, then bent it forward and downward at an angle unachievable by terrestrial frogs. Its mouth had opened then, in a manner difficult to describe, even for Daniel who had been its only eyewitness, and the suckerfish nature came forth.

With saliva dripping from each knife—some of which was beginning to crisscross Daniel's face—the frog continued to speak. "Don't start pontificating about the intricacies of the hemoglobin molecule in order to prove that no life is in the blood. Even the Son of Guile conceded that, and his words are non-truth truth in a world with Despair and Untruth as the pervading forces.

"Let's go on a ride, shall we?"

And in a moment, Daniel's consciousness was engulfed. He no longer saw the macabre display splayed in front of him as he lay on his back but found that he was standing in a cream-colored void with the frog a dozen feet to his left.

He found himself in control of his faculties. If he had been able to remember, it was exactly how he was used to being able to move. All he could fathom at this point was that his movements were different somehow.

He swiveled his torso, looking about his surroundings. There was the frog, which looked smaller, but Daniel was not entirely sure of this point, having no standard upon which to judge his size in a new universe of milky white and tinnitus-like ringing in his ears.

"Are we, are we out?" Daniel ventured to ask, turning to face his captor.

"Hardly," said the frog. "No, you're having a vision, and I am partaking in it. We're still there. If you were to snap out of this vision, you would find yourself still lying in my bloodletting trench in my Oubliette, and I would be perched over you with my knives ready to drain you. None of those realities have been altered, but everything I tell you is, of course, the blackest level of falsehood."

"What? What?" Daniel cried. "What hindrance can you possibly show me anymore? I will die, whether it will take place when you stab me with your knives or whatever you're planning to do, or whether my life functions cease on their own. The only carrot you can dangle in front of my nose is that you will let me go, and I know you never will!" Daniel had moved past the thought of even escape being a deliverance for him. For him to escape and reassimilate into the world he once knew was an impossible proposal.

What was there for him? He had been on a journey and had seen unbeliev-
able sights and had been broken, and now the banalities of life waiting for
him seemed even more utterly empty than before.

The frog passed its tongue over its eye, then said: "You're actually
correct. There are no rewards or punishments here anymore. We're past
all that. I'd hoped that you would be able to move past the trivial apelike
system of punishment and reward. No. I want you to do what you're supposed to do because of enlightenment. Do you want to go through the rest
of existence more or less enlightened?"

"Very well. I don't care anymore. In fact, I never have." Daniel began
to walk forward in the void, reflecting that his life for an indeterminate
amount of time had consisted of being in a domain of difficult walking—
the bean had its curious force of gravity and the way it seemed to lock his
body, and now this void, wherein he had no vantage point in which to scale
his movements, so that every step seemed to be a fall downward until he
caught himself on the next step. It was a supremely disorienting feeling. He
was not sure where he was attempting to go, but he did notice that the laws
of distance and perspective did seem to carry in this world; the frog was
gradually shrinking in size as Daniel propelled himself forward.

"Let me put it to you this way, my friend to whom there is no escape.
We are now in a void, as you can clearly see, and at the snap of my fingers,
the void will clear and you will see the truth, as it were. There's a curtain
covering what we're about to see now. We're not really in this place. But I've
been given powers of transportation, and I can show you other dejected
universes such as ours, for, having plugged myself into the network of one,
so to speak, I can access others. Long have I honed my concentration skills
in order to achieve this feat, but, as you can see, I have a lot of time."

"Tell me, or don't, where the torment will be," Daniel said. "You must
know something of the ultimate one that awaits. I'm tired of being teased
with these tangential torments. Turn to me and tell me what you know of
the one punishment that is eternal, one that is more than this gnashing
of teeth in a new outer darkness. I feel the urge to request my closest kin
to dip his finger in water and rub it on my tongue, except for the fact that
water is only a composition of billions of three-atom molecules, which can
hardly offer true comfort. My life has been stolen from me, and I have lived
centuries alone, stuck with you, if you are even remotely trustworthy, and
half that time I was unaware of what I was doing, unconscious. What torment is there left?"

"One," the frog said in response, ignoring. "One is unity. It is that which is—that which is not nothing. That doesn't sound right, but basically you could have nothingness, but then one of anything assures you that . . . but then I must stop myself, for that presupposes that there is an observer which would already be one. Let me think about this one now from a purely counting point of view. One is, you could say, that which is equipotent with a set containing . . . yes, but do you not see how all your attempts to define one presupposes that one already exists, for to distinguish one from even the void, as you tried to do, assumed the void, and the void would be one as well. Is that not correct?"

Daniel took a few steps forward to distance himself even further from the frog, unsure of what the frog was referring to when he had said that Daniel had attempted to differentiate one from the void.

"I don't know what you're getting at," he said. "This seems like an intellectual triviality when we both know what one is even if the words fail us to define it."

"Ah," said the frog. "There's nothing incorrect in what you just said. One. So again, we come across an axiom: one exists, but then you have to define what is existence. Do you see what I'm getting at?"

"I could just walk in this void that appears to go on forever. We could part ways. I no longer care if this is an illusion. I really just do not. I truly do not care. How do I believe your words that this is all illusory? This could simply be another layer of reality. And I've already long since made peace with the idea that there is no escape from reality—I can only transfer from one plane to the next. Let me walk and see what I can find. I'd rather take that risk than snapping back into the Oubliette with you."

"You forget, my friend, where you sit."

"So blood-let me! I don't mind it if that's what it takes to truly bring me here. If this is only a precursor to where I'm really going, blood-let away! I don't care! Do you understand? And we'll work with what comes next!"

He screwed his eyes uptight, confirming in his heart that this was indeed the end. But he could not. No sooner could he think that than he realized, what is the end? There is no end. There is no end. The ages echo. The ages echo, and even in supposing that all existence was a madcap sloughing of primordial matter, that never explained the existence of the primordial matter, the sloughing, the space in which the movement occurred, or any such concept related to it at all.

With contempt, the frog croaked, a great belch that echoed through the nothingness. "Are you ready? Think of this void we currently inhabit as a hub between discarded universes in the Great Splash. I'm about to transport you into a simulation. A world, a universe, not merely a planet. It's really not even fair to call it a universe. Just a mode of being in which one is not existent, and two is the primary engine that generates the world."

"Mode of two," Daniel said. "I'm not sure I understand."

"The mode of existence you know and even the reveries that you've been in—the musings, the concepts, the aliens whose exploits so laughably gripped your public consciousness—built into all of those conceptions, and everything that you could possibly fathom, everything that the axons in your brain could ever think to connect regarding all of them, are dependent and contingent on the concept of one—just the numeral and the amount, simply one. My self, his self, herself, God, Self. Even some of your religions have as their final goal the assimilation of the many into the world consciousness—to achieve one and God. In all my training, and in my emperorship, one is always the starting point. One can either be good or bad, and we are going to observe a case wherein one is bad. One must be shed; one must become anathema. Is there not a continuum of modes of being that were sloughed off from the great ripple? You were in one, but I can traverse many. And I found the two-world (perhaps not two as an integer, but one in which two is the nearest integer) and in that mode of being two serves as the one, so everything is effectively double."

Daniel countered. "So what? You can still just use two as the unit (or two point whatever it is), and then get on the same way."

"I was anticipating that you would think similarly, but your words betray a one-mode-of-being way of thinking. More will be made clear when we actually make the transition.

"Are you then ready? I warn you that you will see beyond the veil of the one, and you will see the two. This should be sufficient, methinks, to convince you to shed all vestiges of thought that you are loved and you are cared for, that you are in any way important to any entity that may have created you. I've been telling you this for eons. Something has hindered you from fully subsuming that truth, so let's see what we see."

The frog took a jump forward, landed with a squish, performed a quick circular turn that culminated in it facing (had Daniel been able to see what the frog saw) the wall of the Oubliette roundabout near the middle where the semi-minor axis trench would have gone, lifted its right front leg, extended his finger, and traced in whiteness (but really, the wall of the Oubliette) a portal—not a perfect circle, not a triangle, not a square—just a jagged circle drawn by a man with palsy. Where its finger traced, an orange glow gleamed through the seam, and by the way it appeared, Daniel, despite the announcement of what was to happen, felt himself pulling in his mind on old images of jailbreak movies and stories in the newspaper of animals escaping the zoo in Central Park. It was all but impossible for him to see an effective door being carved in the wall of a prison and not experience a lightening in his belly of something resembling manic hope.

Only, ultimately, whether he was really escaping from the Oubliette or, as the frog had said, going to an illusion within a holding area while the true frog lay poised over him with living knives at his face, going from one hoop led to another. It was the same conundrum he had experienced in his mind as a child: die in heaven and rise to the next heaven, and since heaven is unending, these passings through concentric hoops are unending.

The frog stopped carving with its finger, having created an opening that would admit its great bulk. As if there were an invisible wall in the vast whiteness that surrounded the two of them, there was in the surface area of the wall a jagged hole through which the same orange light shone, but there was nothing visible beyond. The frog, seemingly satisfied with its work, lowered its arm back and, after getting some potential energy in its legs, hopped into the hole, and Daniel, as though linked to it by an invisible chain, felt his entire body jerk forward into the hole after it.

11

The Two-Generated World

This author is not thinking of one as a mathematical entity—whether as a unit of counting, or any other such thing. He is positing the concept of one as a vanguard against *le néant*, which, as the author has already alluded to earlier, is itself on ontologically shaky terrain. A window into the nothingness that is *le néant* would theoretically give the observer two distinct cases of this vanguard: 1) the window, and 2) the nothingness itself. But then this would pose a logical contradiction of terms, for the nothingness cannot itself be both one and not one.

—From the unpublished writings of philosopher Constantin Delargy

IF HIS CAPTOR WAS to be believed (except that everything he told him was apparently a lie) Daniel was standing and facing forward into the illusion of the two-world. His mind and eyes were hazy, struggling to take in his surroundings. He was standing, yes, and the world was wavy as if teeming with heat ripples. There was a light greenish-yellow that pervaded the entirety of his periphery. Because of the hint of green, the color was not exactly the same as the cream-colored void he had been standing in before being rudely tugged through the crude orange portal. Presumably, that meant that he was truly in another place. There were objects that were doubtless a landscape, but his eyes were slow in loading.

Where was the frog? And a corollary: if the frog were gone, was he free? Was he, Daniel Lawrence Blythe, free? Could he live here in this new mode of existence alone and unencumbered? He had become so accustomed to living without drinking or eating that those considerations did not immediately come to his mind.

He took a step. His motor skills seemed familiarly normal in this light green ripple of a world, so he began to walk. A portion of him knew that the frog was nearby. Something told him that he was not free from its attention, and that any moment its taunting voice would proclaim itself in his head again. Still, it was nice to be even under the illusion of being out of the frog's sight. It was pleasurable to see a different environment and new colors that were not the mad oil slick of the Oubliette. Daniel squinted as he walked, feeling tears come to his eyes as he basked in the simple joy of seeing a new color scheme. In amazement, he allowed the tears to stream down his face—as clean-shaven as it had been the night of his stealing away—and collect and fall as drops from his jawline. Being so unused to such a simple yet prominent experience, he pondered anew at exactly how the Oubliette had been able to keep his body and its biological processes in stasis, all under the purview of a strange gravitational property that hindered his movements and made it impossible for him to cry and difficult to swallow. All of those curious bodily ailments were appreciably absent in the two-generated world, whatever that exactly meant.

He thought he could make out what looked like trees far ahead of him—a darker shade of green than the rest of the surroundings up against what he took to be the sky. The air felt moist and oppressive. It reminded him of a jungle, the key difference between what was popularly imagined to be a jungle and what he found himself in now was that he was engulfed in utter silence. His footsteps made no sound, and his breathing made no sound. Curious with this, he put a hand to his ear and snapped his fingers and heard nothing. He vocalized aloud and heard nothing.

Daniel was standing still in his tracks, trying to decide if the lack of auditory stimuli was something wrong with his ears or if it was a feature of the world, when he heard the frog speaking in its voice in his head. He turned ninety degrees to his left and there the old beast was, sitting on its hind legs in position number two.

Daniel was not entirely certain, but he believed the frog's slow closing of his hideous left eye was meant to be a wink for him.

"The reason that you can't hear is because you don't have a double. This is the two-generated world, after all, and to poor singletons such as ourselves there are no sounds to be heard. There have to be two entities to hear properly. So, you're only hearing your half of things, as it were, and since you have no double, you hear nothing at all."

I have two ears, Daniel wanted to say. He wasn't sure if he could communicate telepathically with the frog in this realm or not. He tried it anyway. "I have two ears," he thought, tapping into the same brain channels he had always used back in the Oubliette proper. The frog did not seem to respond back to that sentence and instead said:

"Just wait. The features of this world are still being built for you. My simulation is serviceable, but it takes time. Anon, we shall see what a world of two looks like in all its double-generated glory."

It was odd to see the frog so mobile. Though it was the size of a small car, here it moved no differently than a common leopard frog. Daniel figured it must have been tapering its jumps to be able to keep up, for he was walking as a man walks.

The world continued to be a mass of shades of green, hazy, with no other discernible landmarks or edifices of any sort. Being in the Oubliette had caused Daniel to become conscious of his hands and his arms, since, due to the gravitic anomalies of the place, he seemed not to be able to move them well. That conditioning carried through here, because, as the frog had said, he knew he was still in the Oubliette. Yes, his physical body was still anchored there. It was his mind that was allowed to drift to this simulation, this other world. As he walked, Daniel noticed that something odd was happening with his hands. He would look down at his right hand swinging in and swinging out in his gait, not quite as normally as it had looked during his twenty-nine years on Earth, but close. And though his neck was turned to the right, he felt that he began to see flashes of his left arm stamped in his vision and in his brain, but no sooner did he attend to it that the sight before him was his right hand once more.

Yes, that was his left hand because of the position of the thumb and the way his fingers curved in, but he was looking to the right! He was certainly looking to his right. He tried it again by turning his head to the left. His left hand swung back and forth as he stepped, as reliable as the sun was once. Step. Swing. Step. Swing. Flash of his right hand in his vision and mind. Neck never turning. Flash back to the left hand.

By now Daniel had been so conditioned to macabre and unusual occurrences that he was not afraid of the phenomenon with his hands. It was merely something to remark and ponder upon when possible.

Up ahead to his right (perhaps to his left) the frog stopped, but it did not stop as a lumbering car with its brakes being slammed, but with litheness and poise. Like its small earthly kin, it stopped instantly and full of potential energy, a loaded spring ready to kick off.

"You are, no doubt, noticing on our way," it said, "that the shifts over the past few minutes are becoming much more frequent?" Daniel did not know what the frog meant, but he kept his thought-speech silent.

The misty jungle world loomed over them. They seemed to be going to no particular place. The landscape did not change; there was no small object in the horizon that was gradually getting larger as they approached.

Daniel was thinking that he had gone from a limited prison world to an infinite, featureless world and wondered if a happy medium could be reached. Perhaps the world he had known before—the world containing Sylvia—was just that medium.

As if noticing what Daniel was thinking, the frog asked:

"Yes, it seems very drab and monotonous here, but how many hands do you have? You are alien to this world. But the mechanics of the world are struggling to correct you into their pattern. Your mind is seeing your two hands at times in fits and starts. As one hand, so is two feet. If you were able to see your eyes, your ears, your halves of your ribcage, it would look much the same."

The frog stopped and turned in two tiny jumps to face Daniel, lolling its great tongue out.

"Think about this for a minute. This seems to be utter waste, does it not? There is no conscionable reason for why the world would be this way. This is simply the result of some sort of world generation gone wrong—the refuse pile of some great catastrophe—and you (perhaps me too, although I tell you many lies) inhabited only by happenstance a world where the laws and the configurations melded together more seamlessly. Surely you know as well as I that the world you came from is deeply, deeply broken, and I'm not even beginning to talk about wars and dictators and famines and starvation and pestilences. I'm simply talking about the inner workings, the things that your scientists are hundreds of years away from really getting into. It's all stacked up on billiard balls. To use your phrase that I filched from your mind, billiard balls. For some reason it was always billiard balls, not pool balls."

Daniel had never wanted to attribute such a silly-sounding phrase to the angst that perpetually lay at his heart throughout his life, but there was his phrase again, spoken by another: billiard balls. He fought against the slurring of his voice, as if his vocal cords were phasing in and out of being fused.

Another thought injected into his mind: were the Oubliette and its amphibian master themselves ball-conglomerations? If the Oubliette was truly a pocket universe sloughed off from a cosmic reconfiguration event, as the frog had always seemed to proclaim honestly despite his taunting liar's paradoxes, was there a chance that it (and perhaps by extension everything in it) did not adhere to an atomistic construction? If he had had such a question before, it was buried, forgotten, in one of his Lapses.

As if it were reading his thoughts, he heard the frog say: "One can interpret from the Son of Guile's teachings that atomism is another axiomatic portion of physical existence. Now, I being an incarnate spirit—"

"Enough!" Daniel screeched. "You talk of this world of two as if it's some revelation that's supposed to crush my spirit. But I say this again. So it's a world where two functions as the one in this reality. It doesn't make any real difference. There's still a base. There's still a grounding, and if it's foreign to my understanding, it nevertheless still is. I'm not sure what you're trying to accomplish with this. It's almost as if you're expecting me to do something with this information that I can't determine. Are you trying to break me? Are you trying to get me to see something? What is your purpose here?"

The frog leaped and pounced on him. Its saggy, putrid body pinned him to the green earth.

"I have no purpose. You have no purpose. The universe has no purpose. A world without meaning? I'm showing you that principle with numbers themselves. I've known that once numbers are granted, all sorts of chaotic waste ensue. I've alluded to the fact that there aren't any particular specialties given to some integers above others. You think this is all? That there's the one-world that you know, and the two-world that we are simulating now? How many numbers were there again? You flicked beads on an abacus once, correct?"

Daniel struggled against the immense weight of his captor. It was violating and disgusting to have it on top of him. He remembered with a shudder that, in some sense one layer upward, the frog was essentially pinned over him, too.

"You freak!" he spat out. "This is not impressive to me. Any cut-rate science fiction author could have come up with this. I don't see your purpose."

"And I have just told you that there is no purpose. It's not even a case of being fine-tuned constants that brought about life. Everyone knows that. No, what concerns us here—if you look at this vast, empty, green oblivion around you, this jungle that appears like an earthly Amazon jungle that all the outlines, details and resolution have been taken from—is that you see that there is no bottom to this."

"No, what you've shown me is that if I assume turtles all the way down or billiard balls all the way down, and if you remove a couple of the billiard balls, they're still billiard balls all the way down. You've revealed to me nothing. Nothing."

"Well, you're on the right track with nothing," said the frog. "Pursuing nothing is not a terrible goal here." It suddenly hopped off, hitting and crushing Daniel's wrists in the process. Certainly had gravity and pain and modeling limits behaved the same way as in the one-world, Daniel thought, his ulnae and radii would have been shattered. He was trembling. The frog had never been that close to him before. It was putrid, and it was different than simply taking a terrestrial frog, expanding it to absurd size, and plopping it on him. No, he had had a touch with the occult. It was a shard of the Crystalline Assurance.

The frog hopped over some distance away.

"Let's try something else," it said. "Let's establish some axioms on the world you knew before coming to my Oubliette. We will give the crude label 'one-world' to that world. The number one, we should say, is an abstracted, idealized . . . oh, I don't dislike the term: number one is the generator. We're not saying the Creator; we're not saying the sustainer. We're not saying anything other than that it's the generator. Everything traces itself back to one—even things that are fractional trace themselves to one. There is something that I'm claiming to you, though you may not trust me (I understand—that's admittedly part of my mystique). Everything I am telling you is a lie—right now for instance. True or false? This world, I'm claiming, is a simulation. For that is one of my angelic powers: I am able to generate a simulation of a world in which two is the generator."

"You've told me this already. And I counter-claim that by saying this: we are saying *the* generator which in our language still means a *single* generator which still traces you back to one. So have at it. Try to explain to me that I'm futile; you might be right. It might be futile, but you're not going to tell me that life is futile because of the existence of alternate realities. That's something that the youngest child already knows when we read him a fairy tale."

"You dare compare everything you've been going through for the past millennia—all your reveries and plunging into despair, all your mindless contemplating of the Oubliette's walls, all your exposure to the holy words of the Son of Guile, and now your initiation into this alternate mode of being—to a fairy tale?" The frog was incensed and opened its mouth wide. Danie saw a ripple travel through its throat sac and believed that the frog was attempting to croak, although he was unsuccessful in this sound-dampened, blurry forest.

"I'm not saying it's a fairy tale. I'm saying that we already know that there are alternate realities, alternate worlds. It's wired in us. We know and easily accept them."

The frog was silent for a long moment. Daniel had stopped walking and had planted his feet on the ground, suddenly feeling dizzy and disoriented. They had both been mentally shouting in this empty, fuzzy world. In the telepathic silence, Daniel could almost still hear the echoes of their conversation, traveling outward and attenuating, as if his brain was filling in the missing information that the two-world seemed to lack.

The frog considered in the light green fuzz jungle of utter silence. It spoke:

"Surely, the human mind, however, cannot rest in the preponderance of tales. There must be one true tale running clear through all of them, if there is to be any hope—if there's to be any meaning . . ."

This may have been the only time Daniel found himself inclined to agree with his captor. Sensing that they were about to have one of their long conversations, he sat down—a difficult feat because in movement, both halves of his body tended to want to fuse into each other. Like a snake swallowing its tail was trying to sit down. The two maintained their silence for what seemed to be many slow minutes.

Finally, Daniel spoke. "I agree. I agree. And why you would be entitled to this privileged information that I am about to say, I'm not sure. But you're the only one I have to talk to. Wanting that clear, crystal road through all the tales. Wanting the truth. I sought for that so hard, and that is what effectively drove me crazy. I definitely had friends. I appreciated what they were there to do for me. but I did not want to feel like I had some kind of life other than anyone else—in other words, I didn't want to exhibit special privilege. I don't know. I can only feel what I feel."

He paused. "It's odd. It's unusual the way the human mind works." He considered. "I used to find a sort of kinship with Hamlet. He said, 'Boy, I could be contained in a nutshell and count myself the king of infinite space, if I did not have dreams.' I feel sort of the inverse. I am currently in a nutshell; you have put me in it, and you do not seem to want to let me get out. You do not seem to give me an opportunity to get out. Even were I to die, I'm not sure I would be completely out. Nevertheless, dreams aren't the issue. I want there to be infinity."

And as he spoke, he realized his heart was touching into things that he had allowed to lie dormant inside of himself for a long time. "So whether two is the generator, one is the generator, or if some fraction is the generator—none of that essentially matters to the human heart. I think the human heart just wants infinity, even though the human heart at the same time is mortified of infinity. It's not a paradox I really want to rest in. It's just the way it is. And all those things— thought experiments that I would lie on my bed trying to do—watching the pale blue of the evening turn into the dark blue of the night turn into the black, looking out through the blinds, not sure I was going to be able to face it, trying to think about what did rest at the bottom, what was true, what was something unverifiable? I used to think it was the fact that heat rises. Of course, that's the mind of a child. That can be explained as the clashing of billiard balls, but the stories . . . I felt like I had it. I'm losing it again."

The lobes of his brain were folding in. He confirmed himself again the reason why he knew, for instance, that suicide had never been an option for him: he knew that life was eternal. There was never a question of annihilation. From the instant you blinked into existence your eternal existence was set, whether you reincarnated . . .

The hemispheres of his brain felt as if they were trying to envelop each other like a kangaroo sticking her own head into her pouch.

Maybe if he died here, if his body collapsed under the stress of the universe of the two-world, if his bones shattered as his femurs, both halves of his ribcage, all fused into one so he was this ouroboros of horror . . .

What would happen if he did die here? He was already in mortal danger one level up, it seemed, with the frog's living knives poised over his face in the Oubliette. This two-world simulation was threatening to kill him, and the pain and discomfort certainly felt real. He wondered: if he died in the simulation, what then? His lifeless body would either sit there in the jungle, two steps removed from the life he knew—a simulated jungle within a, by all accounts, real Oubliette, or his consciousness would transcend his body, and he would effectively die and be transported somewhere else. But where? Back alive to the Oubliette under the knives?

The end, the best and ultimate case for him was to find a final resting area in either torment, indifference, or bliss, and be stuck there.

His body was shuddering. The frog was chuckling.

"The two-generated universe—I must confess, I didn't know exactly what would happen to you, but I do see that the simulation works rather well, for your essence is buckling under the strain. Every bit of you that is crying to be generated by one now suddenly has to be generated by two. So, at the very least, the lines of symmetry of your body find themselves impulsively drawn towards each other. Now, will they really collapse into each other? I can't say. I must say I wired into this simulation and into the Oubliette in general the stipulation that I can't kill you, nor can you kill yourself. But it's interesting to watch."

The shuddering continued, leaving Daniel to feel like he was undergoing the chills in the strange tropical air. He also felt something distant inside him. Was it pain? Yes, yes, it was a touch of pain. It was somewhere deep. It was hard even to locate in his body since his body was changing into something Other but yes, it was their pain. His pain wanted to be their pain. The right nostril wanted to fold into the left nostril.

As the moments crawled from one pinpoint in time into the inexorable next, the aching grew.

Daniel began to panic. He thought, Help me out. I need to get back to the one universe. But why? What did it offer? Heaven? Billiard balls were the turtles upon which the one-universe was stacked. What about the two-universe?

He had bluffed to the frog about the generators. He had bluffed about his feelings. And suddenly, Daniel crouched to the ground and his ears were in agony, as if he were in a submarine threatening to implode.

It was an agony without agony. It was the sensation of knowing he needed to be in pain. His eardrums were as one. His nostrils were as one.

He grew woozy as he felt the decreased inflow of oxygen, having half the volume as his two lungs folded into one another across the line of symmetry represented by his spinal column. He fell to his knees which had become one knee, and in deeper recesses of his thought (all of which were finding their doubles and pairing off) he even felt the slippery slope beginning where two threatened to become one, and if two reduced to one that one also reduced to one and that one also reduced to one and so on ad infinitum . . .

The frog was right. There was an insanity about this. There was an arbitrariness about this—so much so that he knew that the billiard balls that had haunted him, the round orbs that, it had dawned on him his entire life, would cause him to lie in bed, his eyes shooting awake at night begging for his life not to be this way, thinking as he got older that he could write the pain away by dumping it into the protagonist of a story and letting it go. None of those strategies worked—for he was finally the protagonist in the story, a grand interdimensional tale, and it wasn't working.

Though he had had every reason to believe that his speech in the Oubliette, in the next level down represented by the cream-colored void, and in the level coterminous with the simulated two-generated world was always a sort of telepathic utterance rather than the vibrations of vocal cords traveling through a medium, he was surprised to hear his guttural voice modulating in and out of the familiar pitches of his own sound, possibly due to his vocal cords contracting and smashing into one and then phasing into two again.

"You're killing me. You are killing me. You are killing me!"

The frog in its same bloated corpulence was emitting a curious sound that pitched up and down oddly due to the Doppler effect that was a consequence of Daniel's eardrums struggling against the universal impulse to become one. The curious sound was one laughter, thin in the ether between their minds because it was not two-laughter. Daniel was hearing the frog's laughter not completely succeeding at bursting forth in this simulated world.

"I assure you that you won't die. You don't have to believe me. I wouldn't blame you for not. You don't. There is no trust here. I'm going to stretch you, smash you, and flay you to the breaking point. You must be broken. Yes, you really must be broken. Remember? The trench? The trench. The trench is really your resting place; you're not going to rest here in this double-generated farce. But take its lessons. Take the lessons of a reality in which the numbers themselves that you so tightly clung to don't know what they want to be. This conundrum is the very reason that you're not feeling as much pain as you might. It's because your pain nerves have been reduced to half; you're folding in on yourself."

And then the frog said the words that hurt the most. "And I assure you it's still billiard balls all the way down. Just in pairs."

Daniel was on his hands and knees on the blurry greenish undergrowth, his brain struggling to form coherent thoughts as his very neurons and axons struggled against unicity and merged in and out of phase with each other.

Billiard balls all the way down. But in pairs. The air was made of these billiard balls, and every oxygen molecule was some sort of unit—the two atoms functioning as one. But then the very concept of a unit was anathema to this type of reality, so that the air was a kind of violent dance of contradictions. If he were shrunk down to the level of an oxygen or nitrogen molecule, what kind of unearthly horrors would he be able to see?

And then a thought occurred to Daniel that had never before.

Here, in this two-generated world at least, it was not as if billiard balls clumped together in discrete outcroppings forming stop signs, trees, telephone poles, katydids—assuming such things, or their equivalents, existed somewhere in the vast haziness. No, this had to be a reality of contradictions just barely scraping by without negating themselves by illogic. That was an inescapable conclusion by pondering on the nature of how air must be here—the two becoming the one, the one rejecting itself for not being the two.

But he had spent his entire mature life worrying about how everything in his universe was atomistic, when he in fact did not think clearly about everything being in such a state. He had largely neglected the nature of air.

This could not have been a foreseeable plan of the frog's for, writhing as he was in curious two-generated world agony, these thoughts gave him new insight as he realized that the air separating conglomerations of billiard balls was itself a conglomeration of billiard balls. To suppose that he could somehow separate the viewing medium, seeing those billiard balls without himself being subjected to the influence of them, was rubbish. There was no soaring through empty space to see vast constructions of atoms forming the familiar sights of the life he knew. The medium through which he soared was itself part of the construction, and he could not honestly shrink himself down to the level and get an accurate picture of the microscopic reality.

He felt that he was getting into a seam of something in his mind, and he pushed further, even as the pressures of the two-world made themselves known in his flesh, which was threatening to implode upon itself. It could not be the case that an observer could see the billiard balls. It was not an accurate analogy to say that the world he knew was made up of children's building blocks; it was folly to imagine himself separately surveying.

The billiard balls produced the medium in which the billiard balls could even be comprehended. And to travel from one place—one monolith of balls to the other—was to travel through the billiard balls themselves. Dear God, he had pictured it all wrong. He had fixed it all wrong in his head for most of his twenty-nine years.

No, no. He was part of the system, and the separation was part of the system, and the system was part of the system, in almost an infinite regress. And while infinity was not realized, its conception made its way into the system. The fact that the system had to (or could) ponder different conclusions about itself in order to make sense of itself was a testament to the complexity of the system, no matter the number of generators.

This was something different. What was happening? This two-world was squeezing truths out of him like a lemon. He realized that to say that "billiard balls all the way down" itself—a mockery of the turtle paradigm—was wrong. He would come away from this moment not having all the answers, but he knew he had had a moment. This moment—he tried to hold on to it—he knew that it would fade and possibly find its rightmost extremity, tug on it, and collapse into itself like everything else was threatening to do in this overarching illusion. This was a pivotal moment, but to call it an epiphany would be an exaggeration.

Daniel was still perched on his two (or one) knees and had the sense that he had just landed there after jumping from a high tower of load-supporting turtles. The infinite regress was not truly infinite in this case. His two lips kissed the ground, then fused into one lip.

The frog saw this, saying: "I can sense something. Is that half of joy that I can feel exuding out of you?"

Daniel was glad, despite the circumstances, that his words could express forth without the need of his mangled vocal chords. There appeared to be a mode of communicating with the frog that was their typical telepathic link and one that was their paltry sounds trying to fire in the chaos of the two-generation. "Joy is something I've found hard to come by, in all my life, really. I think what's happening is this: I think your scheme here isn't working. For I am the ultimate escape artist. You kill me here, I just appear somewhere else. I know this in my deepest soul. I can't ever cease to be. And that's not to say that I couldn't end up somewhere I don't want to be, but my essence is not leaving. Nor is yours. So what you are really trying to threaten me with is inherently doomed from the outset. I just had to see it.

"I don't know what your aim here is in this two-world. Whatever you want to call it. This grand and vague gesture around this greenness."

"Nothing. There is no aim. And the reason you're seeing nothingness is because we're seeing half of this world. The other half is out there and, if we were to see it in its proper context, we'd see that this is only half, and the other half would link together with what we do see and give the full resolution of the imagery, and the dimensionality would receive its full effect. You're hearing stereo with one speaker shorted out."

"Perhaps. Maybe. Fine. You're telling me that this is an illusion, so it's unclear to me how faithful all of what I am experiencing would really be to such a world. That's no matter. That's no matter. Thank you. Thank you. You've greatly helped me. The manner in which you have helped me is exceedingly rich."

Daniel then did something that surprised even him. He clasped his fingers behind his head, lay down on his back, relaxed as if he were on the beach, and closed his single eye.

12

Scrambled Denial in Outer Darkness

When one pontificates on God's doings pre- *creatio ex nihilo*, the natural implication (at least, the natural implication in the mind of this author and presumably others) is that all was darkness, save for God and his angels and the demons navigating in some vacuous reality inaccessible from the darkness. The reader is strongly encouraged to expand his perception. He is invited to recall that darkness is a created thing. Darkness is not a non-thing. To say that God's domain and the interplay of the Persons of the Trinity was nestled in a sea of darkness before the impactful words "Let there be light" were uttered is to say, with blasphemy, that *creatio ex nihilo* never occurred. No, the outer darkness yet hangs its existence on its Creator.

–Excerpt from *Fringe Theology* by Erwin Pottsdam, ThD (from D.L.B.'s
private collection)

DANIEL REMEMBERED BEING SIX years old and waking up on one singular morning, climbing down the rickety bunk bed that stood in the corner of his and his sister Ayla's room, being careful not to disturb her. They slept at slightly different schedules, and in true domino fashion he often did wake her by shaking the entire bed as he lumbered down.

This time he was quiet. This morning, he was peaceful and contemplative. Ayla did not stir. It was six, perhaps half past six, in the morning, and the entire house was quiet. He did not even hear his mother or father downstairs. For a few moments, the universe was his. Light made a beam through his window and illuminated a section of the floor, and in the still hour of the morning, the beam of light was almost a yellow and tangible object that he could have cut with a knife.

As he often did, he noticed the motes, the specks floating in the yellow swath. He knew that something powerful was at play in his eyes, and he remembered hearing of God. Genuflecting on the floor and shutting his eyes, grooving them up tight, he dared himself to say one phrase in his mind: The Word was God.

To his young mind, the dust specks in the light dancing in a chaotic pattern were something constituting what he would later just recognize as ultimate reality.

It made sense. Houses were made of bricks stacked up in a pattern. His own body was made of little bits of skin with holes and little hairs coming out of the holes. The same with his dog. Fish were made out of scales. Interlocking objects were made of smaller objects which were made of smaller objects.

The question was: how small did one go before you stopped?

The night before he had lain awake, contemplating the new word he'd learned: eternity. He had heard his sister Ayla breathing peacefully below him. He was glad, given that eternity existed, that someone else was in the room with him.

For forever and ever, ever, ever without never having a stop? Never reaching a determined end? He had thought about that a while, and his stomach wrenched, and he stared at the ceiling above him, and the dark was not totally dark because of the lamp, and he truly had to lie there and wiggle his feet to make sure that he was real. Because some part of his mind had thought: there's no way this is really the world. No, no way. This is really false; this cannot be. This is not real. Nothing is like this. This does not match anything I've ever seen.

His young mind was saying, properly translated, there is no known mundane equivalent for this. I cannot imagine it. I was not designed to live this way.

His stomach rankled. Beaded sweat pooled in the small of his back. He wished his parents would come to him, but he, even at that young age, realized that he was not sure that he needed soothing; he needed this reality to go away, and soothing would not fix it. He needed them to stop. No, he needed there to be a stop. An eternal capital S stop. A stop that would forever hold back the eternal, onrushing tide of the absolute.

And so on the morning when he saw the dust motes in his room and the sun-illuminated scatterers on the floor, and as his eye trained from the floor to his desk littered with nubs of pencils, trading cards, and other miscellany, then behind him again to see his sweet sister peacefully slumbering in her small bunk, he tried to convince himself that maybe eternity also goes on backwards. Maybe there is no smallest. Maybe you can cut these specks in half. You could even stand on one of these little pieces if you were small enough. See the little pieces upon the pieces. See a world contained on one of the little pieces, upon which another world is placed, and on and on . . .

For the first time in hours or days—time had little meaning anymore—Daniel remembered that while he was lying on the earth in this hazy green void, the world of two, with the frog crudely hopping near him in the same general area, he was simultaneously lying flat in the Oubliette's trench with the frog hovering over him—its mouth wide, those cruel organic knives pointed at his face. He was not sure if he was frozen in time up there or if that existed concurrently in another plane of reality. But somehow, he knew that those two events were occurring at the same time and that he was playing two roles.

The frog, as if sensing his shift in thought, said, with a smile in its voice: "I can tell you're thinking back to what's truly happening in the true world. It's funny that it took me of all beings to teach you the truisms of ultimate reality. There are many; I know all but perhaps one or two. But as I've said, one of them is that the life is in the blood. This is a saying that hemoglobin and plasma sera do not capture. No, the life is in the blood, and the words echo throughout the aftermath of the Splash. And when I take out a bit of your life by letting your blood, I will then inhabit your body."

"What's keeping you from doing that?" Daniel snapped. He sat up, and in a lazy attitude he crossed his left leg over his right knee in a figure-four pattern. "What's keeping you? You're telling me your plans. You're telling me your schemes—your ultimate design for me. Whether I believe it or not is another matter, but you're telling it to me. What is stopping you?"

The frog seemed to ponder that question. Finally, with a sickening, wrenching sound it opened its lips again.

87

"I'm telling you this because I need (paradoxically) to be perfectly honest with you, which is very much anathema to me.

"'The life is in the blood' is a truism, but that is not to say that it is the ultimate truism. There is no order that I'm aware of. Another truism, another ultimate axiom, one that can't be proved, one that is an upscaled version of your old childhood 'cold air sinks, hot air rises'—it is the true manifestation of that quest of your mind so long ago, when you were so young and naive—is that ultimate conquering cannot happen unless the conquered to be is fully surrendered.

"When will you fully surrender, Daniel?"

Daniel felt a jolt and, despite his front of looking relaxed and at peace, felt a troubling twinge deep in his breast. That was the first time in all these eons that the frog had used his given name, and it caused him to listen more attentively.

"You're telling me I haven't ultimately surrendered? Look at me!" He gestured in a sweeping motion all around him. "Look at me! I'm relaxing on the ground of a dead world that doesn't even fully process in my mind. My knees are wobbling in and out of phase. My hip bones are trying to become the other one. I'm folding in on myself like a piece of origami, and even this is just a layer removed from the mothership, as I'll call it, where you're sitting perched ready to kill me! I know that when you do kill me, or if you kill me, (I can't sort it out) then I'll go somewhere else that I'm not. I cannot be annihilated. I understand. You know that. So how have I not ultimately surrendered? What hope do I hold out?"

He felt warm tears slide down his eternally shaven face as his voice broke at the last few words. "Tell me how I can possibly have hope?" It was ultimately immaterial if he displayed bravado in the face of the frog or not. His amphibious tormentor held all the chains and was in complete charge of his torture.

The frog said: "I have a sense for these kinds of things, and I sense that you have hope. I don't wish to speculate on it. My job is to find that rogue cluster of hope down inside you, squish it, and lick it up with my frog tongue. And then we'll be ready. This world of two did not seem to work very well. You seem to have engaged in some kind of enlightenment here.

"Yes," Daniel muttered monotonically, doubting vehemently that such a "rogue cluster" was present inside him. "I thought of some things I'd never thought of before. I had always pictured the reductionism of little balls, or billiard balls as I've always called it. But I realized that you can't look at the billiard balls without being a billiard ball, and so I've lost it now, but I had a moment of clarity where it seemed to make sense, and I had a good feeling of how that would actually work and it gave rise—"

"Yes, I would dare say," interrupted the frog with a great clicking sound. "Yes, I'm prepared to say then that the world of two didn't work, and though my illusory powers start to spin out as I get into higher numbers, I'm going to yet try something else. I need you to ultimately surrender. I need the life in your blood to be drained. Let's see. Where should we go next?"

The surroundings went dark.

Daniel sensed that this was the last he would ever see of the two-world (and ended up being correct). Still, he felt a little negative glowing in his breast as he reminded himself that the frog was not gone—he was probably preparing some new funhouse for him. But it was yet good to have some quiet to think through what had been a flash of insight into the world—that the space between the billiard balls, the space itself, was not composed of them, but the very air between the spaces was. There was no air between the spaces, as one commonly thought of air. No, the air was another set of billiard balls, and he almost felt like the Insight was spiraling down the sink, and he couldn't catch it, but he supposed that the lesson of this insight was that you one must be removed from one plane of being in order to critique properly another particular plane of being. It was certainly something like that.

Here he was now in a black void, but he had no mind space even to be afraid. It was interesting how unfearful, how benign the dark seemed when he knew with certainty there were no sharp corners to stumble into, no gruesome bats to land on his head. He was not walking in a straight line that would threaten to veer as his motion grew corrupted by his blindness. Nothing but complete stillness in supernal pitch.

After some radial line of the time dimension had hurtled forward, he began to imagine that this would be like being dead. He knew it was a false fantasy, but he entertained it, nonetheless. What else was he to do? If death included the capacity to allow the mind of the dead to wander forever in a black labyrinth of thought, then maybe he was finally dead, and the fantasy was not false. As he thought about it, Daniel knew that there had to be a mode of being wherein one knew with absolutely certainty that he was dead. Did he have this absolute certainty? Perhaps this was, at last, the Crystalline Assurance.

He knew that his body, as it was, needed nothing to sustain itself; he would be able to run his vital systems indefinitely without need of any outside material, without any decay, without need of any sustenance. That seemed to be either death or advanced suspended animation, but the option of death did not seem so palpable when he was in the pink-and-green-and-yellow oil slick swirls of the great Oubliette. Here, in the decaying dark, things seemed different.

He would be able to shuffle the contents of his mind for ages upon ages. Thinking through the memories of his life, of his parents, of Ayla, of Sylvia. Eric's house with the wood-paneled walls and the discarded bottles of wine and beer. Himself in elementary school. The rabbits scampering out of his way as he walked down the dirt path that opened up into a mile-long trail on his grandfather's property. The sporadic fish jumping out and landing with a small splash in his grandfather's lake. Grandad had been dead for five years; would he eventually wander his way in this dead darkness to find him and reach out and touch his hand again?

The loneliness began to be oppressive. It was not that he missed the frog—it was that he was so accustomed to being his captive that extended time without him felt off.

Only spelunkers into the deepest caves of the Earth truly know what it is like to experience total darkness. The blind have already been discussed as possible epiphenomenological exceptions. All the darknesses Daniel had ever known in his life, having never spelunked, would invariably become slightly lighter as his eyes adjusted, and as they drew in minute sources of light. But this was a dark world where light was foreign. There was no light. He reflected: this was not some kind of cosmic sense of light representing truth and the darkness representing falsity and evil. No, this was merely utter darkness. Utter, outer darkness. Mind existing and outer darkness.

Perhaps this was the closest to what he really wanted—infinity and yet being mortified at infinity. If he entertained the idea and pushed that segment of his brain to its limit, it was true, mathematically speaking, that he had a finite number of memories, a very finite number of vocabulary words, and a finite number of known phonemes. He could sit and invent his own languages. He could try to extract every single sense-memory he had ever had in his twenty-nine years of life on Earth. God, he could try to recreate every single bit of literature, television program, and nugget of history he had ever learned in his life and assign each factoid a twelve-digit code, then he could concatenate each code together into an enormous single integer, then assign a new activity to each digit. He could recite this new number, digit by digit, until they were all exhausted, then he could shuffle every factoid, assign each one a thirteen-digit cipher, and repeat the process. And while it would be true that there would be an infinite number of codes, there ultimately really would not be an infinite number of variety, and so the ice began to grip in his chest and a clenching occurred in his stomach. In particular, it was odd to feel the feeling in his belly because such a sense-impression seemed to be connected to digestion, when he knew very well that food was not required in his belly, which brought back to mind the question if he was sitting here in the darkness dead or not, or if he was even sitting (or standing) at all.

So Daniel pushed back from that site in his brain, back to its center hub, and contemplated a new idea: could he shut himself off? The verdict appeared to be that he could not kill himself (if he were indeed still alive). But could he effectively hibernate? Could he live out endless ages forever in a low power state?

That idea had some appeal. In fact, he envisioned being able to hoist himself over the wall of eternity from time to time—come back to himself after eons of hibernating in order to pat his elbows and rub his knees, to make sure he was all in one figurative piece, then return into the nether-world from whence he had come.

Two words stood out from that hypothetical pathway that let him know that it was a doomed endeavor: time and himself. As the non-sound echoed and whispered past his questionable center of mass in the black-ness, he had the primal sense that he was outside of time, that this darkness was the manifestation of the state of being removed from time's shackles, whatever that meant, exactly. And as time went on, him noting the utter and damnable paradox, he worried that he was losing himself to the void. But he had to wonder: was that undesirable?

Maybe this was truly hell.

He remarked to himself that he had never understood what the gnash-ing of teeth really meant. Weeping he understood well, having experienced the inability to do so during his entire sojourn in the Oubliette, save for the one anomalous time in the dizzying, green two-generated jungle. He had never known people to gnash their teeth in times of distress or darkness. Darkness seemed to be a more primeval fear that one would stand amidst in quiet awe and trembling. If hell was it, and this was hell, and the real-ity of his eternal destiny was hell, then he must prepare for an eternity of darkness, loneliness, and the mind replaying codes of thought throughout endless ages, feeling the time, knowing with a sort of halfway sense that trillions upon trillions of years to the trillionth power were passing and had yet to pass; he would be alone—there would be no getting out, there would no enduring through.

His heart and his chest felt shredded as he said aloud: "I'm in hell. This is it." He had expected there to be more fanfare as he was welcomed in, with God poised angrily above him. He would look up at God to see the displeasure on his mighty face and his great thumbs-down in the Roman gladiatorial sense, and he would know he was being shuffled off to darkness—eternal darkness without ever rotting or his thought-dreams being annihilated.

Billiard balls in the air. Billiard balls are the air. Not in the air. They are the air. And to see the billiard balls as they are meant to be seen requires one to . . .

The truism he knew (whether he believed it or not) was that God was good. God, he had never really entertained the idea in his mind, ever given due diligence to consider the question of whether hell was unfair or unjust. He mused that he mayhap would have ample time to think about this as he pulled out all the drawers in the card catalog of his mind for all eternity, endlessly iterating, endlessly being reminded of the finitude and the tedium.

It was not a question of whether hell was just or unjust but a more encompassing detail: was God just or unjust? And if God (and so hell) was unjust, then God would do precisely what Daniel thought was happening to him. God would unceremoniously shift him from life to the outer darkness through subterfuge. One moment he would be walking—perhaps down a small town road at night almost deafened by the cicadas, hoping that skunk spray that he smelled was not fresh, and there was nothing else lurking around, and the next moment he would be rounded up, rudely cuffed, and shoved into the paddy wagon of hell that he was in currently.

Daniel remembered, though, that unlike the Egyptian scene of the underworld, the Aztec scene of the underworld, all the scenes of the underworld he had seen in books, the Christian view of the underworld had a major difference in that the sentencer gave each subject an unambiguously fair trial. In his life, he had never mused much upon that, nor put himself behind the eyes of a hypothetical damned one entering hell, but this cloistering darkness seemed a good place to do such ponderings.

He had no inkling if this thought process was taking years, centuries, or milliseconds. It all collided together.

The ultimate power, the Ultimate Creator of the Universe consigning certain of his creations to an outer darkness—let us assume that is a given.

There was quite a tension taking place between all the constituents of this Gedankenexperiment. If this creator claims such a process is just, then it is just by fiat, because no one else can reasonably exist to object. But from that it would seem to follow that it is not entirely fair, because he gets to set the standards. There seemed to be lining up in the ruts of this argument the preparations for his old favorite—an infinite regress. What would be the more just action: the paddy wagon or the revealing and then the subsequent sentencing? None of these straggling strands were easy to reconcile. It was not easy to decide by virtue that the subject of the thought-experiment was by definition the grounds of all thought itself.

Daniel imagined standing before the great Head of God, laid bare and knowing with Crystalline Assurance that he would be sent to a place of torment and knowing that he would be in that state of torment knowing the face of God. Being in hell with that memory forever engraved on one's mind would only seem to add to the torment, would it not?

Some time ago, he believed himself to have said the words aloud "I'm in hell." Had he? Did he hear? Could he think, or were sounds and images merely being generated in what passed for the uppermost quarter of his body? Did he have a mouth? He reached up his hands to touch his lips and realized that he had no hands and nothing to move. He had no head; there were no ears to hear sound. All the bodily illustrations that had passed through his mind for the time immemorial he had been in this darkness were functions of the anthropomorphic nature of his brain. He had no organs nor no body parts; he was a disembodied mind floating through a black void.

I know, said either his mind or the automaton standing in for it in the darkness, that none of this is entirely true either. Because what he took to be his real body, somehow prolonged and kept alive unaided by the need of familiar nutrients and minerals, was in reality (he believed) lying flat in a trench with knives—but not metal blades forged from the raw materials of the earth. No, metal blades produced from the interior of an alien or demonic frog. They were poised at his throat, and he was in some sort of trance, some sort of illusion. What was it for? What was the purpose? Why was this happening?

He struggled to remember this strange theme of honesty while un-speakable horrors were being produced. His imagination ran through the scenario of the face of God's sentencing centers—a doomed sinner at least gaining a glimpse of the great face before making the unreturnable plunge downward into hell. Did all this lie in store for him yet, or did the future have any appreciable meaning anymore in this outer darkness?

The demon was still not being completely honest with him, despite the frog's purported need to be so. The very reason he had ever been captured from his Arkansas home and put in the Oubliette and the ultimate reason the frog wanted him at all—in eternity he would have time to wonder about this. But he was falling at the moment, despite the absence of any ground rushing up at him, and he decided it was time to catch hold of the ledge in the darkness. He was not really in the darkness. He might be in here for some time to come, but he was not really in darkness.

And his fingers caught hold, and he was able to rebuild a small sense of himself with that Crystalline Assurance: there was an I in this darkness, and that I was coterminal with Daniel Lawrence Blythe. So reforged, he thought further.

Let us assume that an entity has arranged for himself somehow, maybe through an unknowable process, maybe through some kind of combat, to sit in the grand universal seat as supreme judge.

The ultimate judge: his ways are inscrutable to his subjects and through arbitrary means and standards his sentences are carried out. Let us surmise that a subject's sentence begins from the premise that all are sentenced. Gradually, some sentences can be commuted, but others stay attached when the court season comes to a close, and this is a final close with no hope of reopening or appeal. The poor people whose sentence is not commuted by the judge receive formally their sentencing at the very end, and they get a glimpse of the judge before they are sent to their final resting place, except there is no resting involved in this endless torment beyond imagination.

The question almost poses itself: Is such a judge fair?

The question itself is perhaps a poorly posed one, because fair implies fairness implies submission to a standard, and this judge, being the ulti-mate judge, sets the standard and in fact, embodies and is the standard. But then, is the judge fair? In asking such a question with such premises, the question morphs into a different question: is the ultimate judge consistent with himself and, being the infinite judge, is the ultimate judge unable to make a mistake or to be inconsistent? The answer to that question is, of course, a tautological Yes.

So what questions were left to ask?

The question lay in the nature of the sentencing. Does the nature of the sentencing ring with what they would consider good or fair? Because fairness from the point of view of the subjects is rather arbitrary.

From his invisible handhold, Daniel was going through the vast recesses of the darkness. He knew himself, but that was increasingly all. His mind asked these questions (which he suspected were starting to unravel, not unlike when he underwent the Lapses at the top level of the Oubliette) and at the same time another low furrow of his mind was playing out a possible future with Sylvia, exhausting all codes and exhausting all words that he could, exhausting all false memories of a life with her.

Shuffle the genetic material, have two phantom children with her. Live those days out. Reach the end until whichever person died first and then the deck was shuffled anew in the darkness, and a new world awaited in which Sylvia was his again.

Begin again.

While it would be an easy estimation to say that he would have infinite variety, and thus he could potentially revel in an infinite amount of possible futures, he yet felt, sitting in this darkness, that it was not technically true that it was an infinite amount of possibilities—that the only infinite possibilities he could truly have were banal infinite possibilities, such as having an increasing number of children, or on a world with three moons rather than two, things like that.

Not true infinity.

The nature of the judge reveals his face. Even though the sentencing is a foregone conclusion, he reveals his face at the end. Does he do that to look upon his creation one final time before plunging them into the abyss? That did not seem likely. He can see them at any time; he never loses sight of them. He himself being consistent with himself would not be able to lose sight of them at any time.

The great Head of God appears over the edge looking down on his creation, hammering the gavel and directing them to their chute, and they see him.

They see him before they are lowered down.

Will they remember him down there? He wondered.

It was not so easy to say. An argument could be made either way. However, it is called a punishment. And amnesiac punishment would certainly not be as effective as a punishment knowing.

In all situations, seeing this ultimate judge—being presumed the ultimate good—would be a cause for reverence and awe. In this case, having a memory of him in the flames . . . it would not be a positive memory to cling to.

To endure in the pit.

There is no enduring. You would hold that image of his face in your mind for all eternity. Looking over the rim of the pit as you are lowered down, and you know that his disappointment and sadness in you is unending.

On the contrary, if another entity not proclaiming to be the ultimate judge abducts me and takes me from all that I know, and in a paradoxical way tells me that he is lying to me, is it not the case that the very fact that he is contrasting to me truth and falsity shows that he lacks in his very presence the Crystalline Assurance?

And what is the Crystalline Assurance? he wondered. He had heard various permutations of its meaning over his sojourn in the Oubliette and its offshoot worlds (even now he was beginning to wonder how long he had been in the darkness as a function of bodily cycles, which he lacked anyway). To him, it was the indescribable feeling without being a feeling that one was in the presence of absolute Truth. One could doubt even billiard balls. But the Crystalline Assurance was so-called not because of some kind of rigid atomistic structure, but because of the firmness of the Truth it conveyed.

To be in the presence of Truth and know that something was incapable of being doubted, because the feeling (that was somehow not a feeling) that emanated from it was self-evidently veracious!

He felt that he had almost had a shard of it in the two-generated world, pondering as he did about the air itself being billiard balls flowing through the other billiard balls. And something was scratching at his heart just now, even thinking as he was on horrid and murderous things. A judge sending the majority of the constituents represented by his court to unendurable damnation, but a judge easily capable of commuting sentences by merely the proper appeal to the court. Could such a thing be right? Could ultimate reality—Great Splash or not—be structured in such a way that even one minute corner of the On (whatever that exactly meant) behaved in that way? Was that right?

But in that moment Daniel knew that it was right. And it was just, and his breast swelled as he felt the love of the universe flow through him. He knew that he was not really in the darkness. By contrast, he knew that in the true darkness—if it ever did occur for him—there would be weeping, and there would be gnashing. And so, without one, not the other. The law of modus ponens.

And then finally the words of all he had ever been exposed to in his life penetrated his heart and he believed that he believed that he knew. He chose to believe, somewhat understanding in the dark moment that belief was really a matter of breaking down the wall rather than building anything. He needed to submit and believe what he already knew.

Dear Lord, he said, surprising himself. No, I'll say it, Dear Lord. Not as a salutation in a letter. Not as an opening address and a prayer. Not even a full sentence and agreement with things as they were. Dear Lord. There was a Lord. There is a Lord, and He is dear.

What an odd way to regard him as dear, Daniel reflected, considering the nested layer upon layer of where I am, knowing that I could be in this dark realm and get stabbed and not know it. I could be stabbed one layer up or two layers up (I've lost track) and where will I go next?

But remember me, Dear Lord. Is it true that by acknowledging you as Lord, I'll go to a benign zone? Is there any way of knowing whether I am still alive or not? When do I know I've reached the final resting place, the train having stopped?

The Crystalline Assurance would have come in handy. God, the fact that I am alive (or at least conscious) and can contemplate these things—that I as a member of the universe composed of its elements represent the universe reflecting upon itself. That lends to me a layer far stranger and far more profound than what I am currently in.

And moreover, the space between the billiard balls is itself made of billiard balls, and there is no knowing whether you are part of the motion or above the motion, and when the motion truly ends; all that I really can say is that the ending redounds in the Dear Lord and He is somehow swept up in the motion and yet not part of the motion.

But yet, despite these surges of crystalline feelings without feelings, there was a dark blotch in the darkness. This Oubliette that I find myself in—I am told that there are others, there are other bubbles created from the wake, and it is all nothing but an idiotic splash. I don't think that that is accurate. I think that the lie is revealing itself, and my God, I don't like the dark. I know I'm not in the ultimate darkness (due to the great and mighty law of modus ponens), but I don't like the darkness, and I don't believe that I could ever really rest here, and I don't want my reality to be this way. And I know that I am just like a dark blotch myself. I know—O I know that I'm myself and part of the dark blotch. This is me, and I'm part of this, and I need the dark blotches of myself to be removed. It's not my surroundings. It's me. It's me, and I know that I've done wrong. I know that I am wrong— myself am wrong and I, Dear Lord, I know, and I am sorry. Forgive me.

And then in some undisclosed manner the darkness got darker to such a degree that the darkness he had been in heretofore was like snow.

He thought aloud: You're lowering my guard to make me question what I've just done, but I have just done something irrevocable, or, much more accurately, something irrevocable was just done in me. And I suppose darkness more profound than the deepest cave or the tightest shut eyes is nothing, he mused to himself, because there was light before there was ever a light source according to the Scriptures, and so light did not necessarily mean waves of electromagnetic energy. He ventured to think that such primeval light was truth itself and had a physical representation in his world.

But he was several layers removed from the world he knew, and darkness had a counterpart perhaps equally matched. The question, though he had not long ago felt that he had conquered it and answered it in the firm negative, was: Was the darkness the outer darkness, and was he lost?

Daniel felt panic creep over him. The world was an unavoidable minecart track of assurance and doubt, and each was just beyond the crest of the other. How do I get out of here, and where would I go? Why would I even want to hope to get out of here? Is a small increment of less dark more preferable? He wondered. He mulled over this question for an unspecified amount of time. And right here, in this case, despite all the odysseys he had taken in the millions of years since he had been stolen away into the Oubliette (but everything he had ever been told was a lie), and all the time dilations he felt subject to in the Lapses and in the worlds generated by the frog's powers of illusion, here in the deep darkness it felt the most like time was squashed and not existent. Similar to how his bodily pairs in the two-generated world rankled against the very strictures of the environs, so too did his mind and nonexistent body stretch precariously against the absence of the very engine that gave them the dimension in which to move.

I was birthed from a version of darkness. I was thrust forth onto the Earth without wanting to be and in fact, I know the concept of wanting to choose one's own birth is a meaningless concept, for it is a causal loop in a sense. Yet there I was. And I lived for twenty-nine years, and I experienced joys, and I experienced sorrows, and eventually I tied up all these and more into the fruitless concept of the billiard balls.

And that world is now millennia behind me. I've been caught up in what I now know with perfect clarity is not an alien spaceship.

How could he prove it? And to whom would he prove it? And what was perfect clarity, really, if it was possible to doubt that to which it was pointing immediately and with no challenge?

He could only prove such things to himself, but fear hung over a part of his heart. And as those words transpired in his mind, he had an image of a crystal.

And since his head was no different than the darkness around it (in fact, he wasn't even sure if he was a body anymore), it would be fair and perspicacious to say that the crystal illuminated his head, and there was no demarcation between what was really there and what was just sensory data processed by his brain. The mental image of a crystal glowed, which meant that the crystal was not transparent but in fact had a light source of its own and enough to hang truths upon. The crystal felt to be immense; there was no scale he could measure, being a possible incorporeal mind, and so he could not say the size, but he felt that it was gargantuan, and it was angular and true. And shiny, milky white, and sometimes iridescent white, and sometimes the color of lightning, and he knew that he was not in the spaceship or pocket galaxy of the old frog while it was boasting about its lies, not right this moment, and that the old demon was telling the truth at least about some things.

There were other bubbles of reality beyond just his birthing world and the Oubliette, for he had just been transported to one. He was, temporarily he felt, not in the darkness waiting for the fall of the living knives layers upward. No, he was in a clean realm, where the darkness felt warm and a hotbed of potentiality, and where insofar as it was the color black, it was so because it was the intermixing of all the color pigments rather than the stark absence of any of them.

He asked: Am I me?

He heard back: No, it wasn't. There was again no assurance if they were saying words aloud or only thinking, or if there was even a distinguishable difference between the two concepts. Daniel wondered how the crystal's rejoinder was a logical response to his question.

No, it wasn't?

Are you alive? he asked. There was no answer. But he had in his breast a thrumming similar to the violent walloping that he would feel against the edges of the bean when he got too close, but those kinds of humming were distressing and violating and threatened to split his head into shreds. This hum was equally potent, but he felt within him the ability that, if he had wanted, he could have blasted that crystal into shreds, and he could have used those shreds and torn a hole in the canopy of the darkness that he was in, fashion another shred into a rope that would stretch, and he would swing through like a swashbuckling hero to greater things beyond.

The embodied Crystalline Assurance blasted forth in a still, quiet voice that yet amplified itself in the darkness made perfect:

"In the true ultimate of ultimates, which is irrevocably carved in the On and is itself the On and the On's wellspring and the conduction of the rhythm and the pattern of the music of the On, it will have always been the case that each and every permutation of what is truly and sovereignly bestowed (which is to say, every infinitely regressible atom of the On) is one. So there is an infinite collapsing of the eternal within the supremely uncountable.

"It is not for nothing that your name is Daniel, Denial."

13

Surfacing as Denial

When one reflects on what truly constitutes the purview of the Almighty, one can only fall to one's knees in awe. In a reality where curiosities such as Graham's number exist—a value so large that the known universe does not have enough room to house the digital representation of it—we must be firm in our convictions that God is behind every iota of truth, that God is a great nebula of goodness tucked neatly away behind every twig.

—Excerpt from *Fringe Theology* by Erwin Pottsdam, ThD (from D.L.B.'s private collection)

As DANIEL AWOKE WITH a start, for the most minute of seconds a sort of muscle memory in his brain formed around him the images of more peaceful climes, the surroundings of more genial areas of awakening. Even though as a child he had eventually come to reinterpret the surroundings of his childhood bedrooms as places ultimately hostile to him, being bound to the vicissitudes of time and a reality wherein billiard balls were the unavoidable fate, they were at least safe havens from outside forces.

And even in a half second, he could see the familiar tin rocket ships, diecast cars, and cluttered stacks of books sitting on the old rickety table under his bedroom window where he commonly saw the myriad motes of dust dancing in the air as the sunlight shone through the east-facing window. Amalgamated with that memory was the memory of him in his bedroom at age twenty-nine in his ramshackle rent house—still littered with books but now also with ashtrays, beer bottles, and other detritus.

But no, he had not even been asleep. And he was not in a room. He was still in the Oubliette, and everything was as it was, and the frog was poised over him with the knives protruding from its freakishly stretched open mouth.

Daniel looked down at his hands. They certainly were there. He knew that his hands were clean. And he knew that no blood ran within him anymore. There was no blood to spill into the infernal trench—the blood was still physically present and pumping, but the life in it had transcended and no longer belonged to him. And he also knew that the frog had no more power over him.

Things had so suddenly snapped to that he could scarcely appreciate that he was back, a layer up or down or forward, and there the frog was, mouth poised over him opened with knives gleaming, as it had been doing the entire time he had traveled through the two-generated world and the world of utter darkness.

"All right. We are back," the frog's voice said. A drop of slaver fell on Daniel's face and trickled down his cheek, landing on the soft floor of the Oubliette's trench.

There was strength in his voice as Daniel retorted, "Yes, we're back." He felt that the massive crystal in the darkness had somehow lodged in his head, and he could drape truths over it, and it swelled to fill the inside of his beaten and broken body from his precariously compromised head to the tips of his fingers and toes. And he knew that if those knives were to come crashing on him and puncture his face, they would in some way pierce him and yet crumble because of the hardness of the fortitude within him. That was the crystal's doing and not his.

"We're back. Are you prepared to do what you were going to do?" Daniel asked.

"That depends. Haven't you seen the utter depravity of it all? By my count, you've seen one—perhaps two—botched creations that I can simulate. I'm actually not sure if the darkness you experienced without me was my doing, or if it was merely the scraping between simulations, but everything I tell you is a lie. Rest assured that there are many more, and you know that I know that you can sense this. One is enough to see the threads of the mind begin to unravel. You've already lived in one botched creation by my account for twelve billion years at this point."

The living knives still pointed inches from his face.

Twelve billion years. The commonly accepted estimation back on Earth was that the sun would have been in its final stages. Everyone he had known was long demolished in a time scale that was almost meaningless to him by virtue of its immensity.

No. It was a lie. And even granting that it was true, it was not relevant. He knew the crystal inside of him, which was not really inside of him but through him and over him and behind him, all at once. The crystal inside of him was feeding him the line: it's not true.

"Don't believe it? Well, I am impressed. But in the final end, all I need you to know and recognize is your despair. I need to see the beginning of your loathing of the world and your place in it. How you come by it is immaterial. These seeds are signs of your despair. I need to see these signs before the bloodletting can begin.

"You agree with me, correct?" The frog paused, the entire arsenal of his knives pulsating back and forth three inches or so with each jagged breath he took.

"I agree. I agree. The world is utterly loathsome. And yet I don't know why that doesn't make me despair. In fact, it almost seems to bolster me— the waste that I saw, the chaos that I experienced. None of it was mine to control, and the responsibility for it was dumped on someone else. And I think you know who that someone else is."

The trench in the floor of Oubliette seemed to push a counterforce into his back, and if he tilted his head so that his ear was more towards the floor of the Oubliette, the deafening static noise still wobbled to and fro in his head, but not with the same intensity as when he was initially exploring his prison. Without ever leaving the relatively small dimensions of the bean, he had yet wandered an odyssey within an odyssey within an odyssey, and he had touched at the very deepest part of his descent the crystalline assurance made manifest and tangible. He had the sense that these crystals were always there—they were in everything. Just like the beast in his story, the hideous wretch in his dream with the nail-like appendages hammering out of his head, these crystals were always there, just outside the bounds of conscious perception, and these crystals were not really crystals, but guardians of some kind—angels, even—that had assumed the form of a crystal for his benefit.

The complete absence of doubt and total, unimpeachable assurance—it was curious to ponder over. It was curious that he was even pondering anything in the situation that he was in and not cowering in utter fear. He felt a confidence such that he had a mastery of the time in the Oubliette itself, having surfaced from the dark world a victorious, if not still doubtful, conqueror. Possibly the frog was not perched there, statue-still with knives pointing downward, on its own volition, but he (Daniel) was effectively freezing time in order to gain more space to be able to figure out what to do.

Did he not think that the crystals were some kind of entity or deity?

No. He had called out Lord. There was Lord and Lord only. The crystals were some kind of representative of the Lord, and he felt the golden sweet swelling in his breast as he thought about the tantalizingly brief moments in the crystal's presence when doubt was gone. It was almost laughable even to consider, and he could not possibly carry that thought and that feeling back over to another land. He was there, and it was localized only there. But it was there, and he had felt it, and it would be self-contradictory to doubt the reality of a past moment where doubt was a gaping void.

No. It was there. It was there embodied in the crystal, and he felt small hints in his heart that the assurance had been there. It was a marker on the map. And he had touched it, and he had called out, and the Lord had put that thumbtack on the map, as it were, to show him.

So now, where was he? What was his state of affairs beyond the face-value environs of being threatened by demonic knives coming out of the mouth of a grotesque frog creature in an inescapable pocket universe?

If A, then B. If the Lord had reached down or in and had put a thumbtack on the map of his odyssey to show him that he was there, then there was certainly nowhere that the Lord's presence could not go. Daniel, by being in proximity to the crystal in the dark, had experienced being something like a Geiger counter to the absence of doubt—the closer he was to the crystal and the Lord's thumbtack, the hotter was the radioactivity of truth, and the faster came the clicks. If that, then, what did he have to fear from this frog any longer? In fact, the frog's whole hierarchy of plans was utterly revealed to be a sham.

He licked his lips, feeling a little more moisture than he had used to in eons, and spoke.

"I'm prepared to die. I've been in here a long, long time. And whether you can read my thoughts or not, I will tell you that I've always been hesitant to die, because I quite honestly don't know where I'll go, and even if I end up in a vast grotto of flames, lava, stalactites, and torment, I don't truly know if that would be my final resting place just as much as if I had landed in paradise with golden streets and fruits with healing for the nations.

"I don't know if my consciousness is to pass unendingly through a succession of locations, or if I am to be annihilated utterly, and then it was as if I never was. I don't know. I didn't know—let me correct myself. I didn't know. But I do know now, and I don't think this was your goal—my knowing—but it is what happened. And I do know that—"

He paused. It took him the most effort he had ever exerted in the entirety of his short twenty-nine years, but he said it. "I know that my Redeemer lives. And I know that if your knives fall upon me in the next few seconds, destroying my physical body, which is the dwelling place of my immortal soul, then my soul would transcend the boundaries of this bean and rejoin my Redeemer, for there is nowhere that he is not. He was within me and without me in the vast darkness that I experienced, which was the void between your pitiful illusions and a place that you are entirely banished from by definition, rooted as you are in your limited illusory powers. There I grazed the crystalline assurance of his mighty presence.

"But you have assured me, in your confusing and contradictory way, that your aim is not to kill me with these knives poised above my face, but merely to draw my blood. The flaw in your reasoning is that life is indeed in the blood, but my life is no longer in this particular collection of blood that shoots through this hunk of meat that comprises my physical body. You waited too long, and I was able to have a chance to have my life placed in an entirely different and pure supply of blood elsewhere.

"If you were to draw my blood and fill it in this trench for reasons that are still not completely known to me, but rooted in your almighty truism that life is in the blood, all you would ultimately have in this trench would be red, sticky liquid. Red, sticky liquid and a wounded or dying human body. Assuming that I die, I will be somewhere else. I will be with the Lord. And as regarding your Oubliette, I don't know where this is located on the map of all the universe, but I believe that he'll be able to find me. He found me in the deep darkness, the darkness that I believed was my eternal death. He'll be able to find my dead body in here. He'll be able to restore all the blood to my body and return me to my present state, but transcendentally glorified.

"So, what that means for you is that if he finds me, he's going to find you. You cannot possibly be hidden in this Oubliette, not now or on the other side of the end of time."

A different knife stuck upward from the floor through Daniel's stomach. He touched his chin to his chest and saw the bloody tip protruding out of the lower right quadrant of his abdomen.

The frog spoke almost soothingly: "Comfort gestates in the ridges of the worm. Do you remember that, Daniel?"

Daniel's eyes darted over the knives still perched over him as if keeping stock that one had not after all gotten loose and pierced his body. No, the familiar bundle of silver implements, some shorter, some larger, some with serrated edges, were all intact and accounted for.

So, I am finally going to die, he thought, feeling warm tears welling in his eyes as he fought against the racing of his thoughts.

No. If I am going to be gone, I will leave with a sound and stable mind. My friend the frog has powers even beyond what it has demonstrated over my stay in his Oubliette, and it has summoned a hidden knife out of the ether to do me in at last.

It, of course, served him right for taunting the frog. In the next several moments, as the blood drained from his abdomen, filling the trench from the vicinity of his lower back rather than from his facial regions, he would have a chance to see played out the assurance he had so brazenly displayed in front of the frog. He would soon know whether his bold assertions about leaving the Oubliette and escaping to his Redeemer was in fact as true as it had felt—without feeling—in the presence of the crystal, which he hoped still resided within him.

Of a certainty he knew the line "Comfort gestates in the ridges of the worm." It had long been consigned to his deep memory, but as soon as the frog had recited it, even in his tearful state of shock, all context and relevant history had come swooping into his brain as if it had been in the forefront the entire time.

It was when he was sixteen and when he had dreams of selling the perfect story to the short story magazines that for years had cluttered up his room, now separate from Ayla's. *Stories of Wonder. Fantastic Accounts. Bizarre Legends Quarterly.*

And curiously, the pain was miniscule, but, then again, no bodily sensations in the Oubliette had ever been standard.

For one particular story, "Comfort gestates in the ridges of the worm" was to have been his kicker line, part of a short poem that was either said in the mind of a disembodied spirit inhabiting a worm or a true, innocent worm that was allowed by providence to have human thought processes in the instants before his death. Like most of the short stories he had ever started in his life (now coming to an end) he had not decided the ending nor developed the story much beyond this line.

Here, at the end, he was able to say that his life was one vine swing from an uncompleted story fragment to the next one. He had run out of vines from which to swing.

Daniel could remember the genesis of the idea of the story. He had adopted the romantic idea of waking up and jotting down whatever momentous thought was in his mind. It was one night when the forever loop was running rampant in his thoughts, when the angels plummeted forth and down through the eternal fabric, that he awakened and prayed to the emptiness before him that he could find a peaceful pattern and felt himself a small, insignificant cog in a vast and indifferent eternal machine comprised of dumb and insensate billiard balls.

The worm on the very brink of death knows more than I have ever accrued in my entire life, for the only true knowledge worth having in this world is what happens to one upon one's final heartbeat. So, in a very true sense, a common robin can wring out more eternal insight than a lifetime of fruitless study.

Comfort gestates in the ridges of the worm. And now I am the worm and the knife is the robin and my own blood is its gastric juices.

In the story, he was going to trace the acceptance of a lowly worm, an ignorant and instinctual vermiform, who eats rotting material ("I honor the Father with my ingesting of the detritus of a thousand vile deaths") and was itself a prey animal to any number of wild beasts in its habitat. And before the splash of acid rendered him into mush in the stomach of a frog or mouse or robin (he remembered leaning toward the idea of the robin) the worm was to have this epiphany: "Comfort gestates in the ridges of the worm." And there was more, but that was the takeaway line as the story came to a close with hopes of conveying to the reader the importance of accepting his place in the dance.

But as time had gone on, Daniel had come to realize that it was not even the case that there was a confusing dance with unbalanced partners and mismatched feet, poor timing, and off-tempo percussion. His excitement over the grand insight revealed at the end of the story was eventually tempered by Daniel's unwelcome reductionist dwellings.

There was no dance, which was strikingly adjacent to saying that there was no meaning nor no purpose. There really was no dance if all of the observable universe was a mere lumbering vibration of pockets or patches of clusters of billiard balls.

There was no dance.

So had said his younger self. Had he had it wrong? It was scarcely worth worrying about now, for he was soon to leave the world, syncopated or not.

Even in a reality where a Redeemer is superseding, does it follow that there is a dance?

Where am I? What is my state, and when will I cross over? His vision was blurring, whether through tears or fading consciousness, he was not sure. He wondered how much blood he had lost thus far. He was afraid to look anew at the tip of the unforeseen knife coming out of him, so he stared upward at the other set of knives, wondering why they were still in position if he had already been stabbed.

Revisiting memories. Was his life flashing before his eyes as he remembered the worm story? Recollections of looking out through a television set into nothingness.

Nothingness. There was no such thing. So, in effect, nothingness was nothingness. He felt the corners of his mouth tip upward. Hello, old friend Infinite Regress.

Daniel felt at last that the entire universe, all the thousands of cubic meters of the Oubliette, were waiting for him to speak. So he did, but not in the traditional sense, for which he was grateful. He proclaimed forth with his mind just as feebly as he felt he would with his true lips and tongue:

"Yes, frog, I remember those words. And I can do you better:

Comfort gestates in the ridges of the worm.
I freely sate you with my offal.
And know that someday you will reach your term,
For you will fill another beast's jaw full.
And this feast is unending, for at the summit,
A creature will find upon its demise
That it turns fodder for another varmint.
All become nourishment under the skies.

Yes, I'm aware of my story fragment, just as I am in the process of becoming a story fragment."

The frog actually leaned back to give its knobby, warty front feet enough clearance to be able to give three squishy claps.

"Well done, well done! Now, people have many story ideas, even those who aren't interested in becoming writers. But it's curious, isn't it? It's curious that you at one point in your life had the idea of trying to write some story about a disembodied spirit in a worm finding himself in a very tight ovoid enclosure, if I am reading your memories right. A frog was even involved in the tale, was it not?"

Daniel felt too weak to respond quickly. His reaction time was slowing.

Seeming to sense this, the frog beckoned with his front foot in a dismissive gesture. "You may speak, Daniel."

"I don't know," Daniel choked. "Some kind of animal eats the worm at the end, not necessarily a frog."

"I'm sure that in time, had you finished the story, that you would have settled on a frog as the eventual devourer."

"It's funny," Daniel said with a serenity beginning to pool in his gut, "that I didn't think of a more fitting fate for the worm: the barb of a fishing hook. It probably would have given him more time to contemplate his coming end while sitting in the water, knowing that a fish would be coming to eat him. But then again, I would sometimes walk the sidewalk in our town after a rain. I would see all the worms come out, which did inevitably attract hordes of frogs. But, at least where I came from, they were usually toads, and they would feast—"

"Is that how you got the idea for the story?" The frog's voice continued to be cloyingly gentle.

Daniel's voice was in another realm. Was he beginning to feel warmth and dampness in the small of his back? "I don't know. Probably. It was a case of briefly feeling like I knew my spot. I knew everyone's spot. If I were to pick a random person out of all the persons of the Earth I would know his spot in life, and I felt like I was the worm, and I wanted to tell myself that even as I was being ground up or dissolved in the belly of some creature that I was carrying out some miniscule part of a master plan.

"Plus, it seemed that the worm on the verge of dying knew more secrets of the universe than I did. At an infinitesimal instant in time, the worm was the wisest being in the cosmos."

The frog pushed in. "And are you a worm now, with a stomach full of rotting material? And are you on the verge of death? I have truthfully told you that you aren't. It wouldn't do for me to kill you, as I've said. Only to blood-let you."

Daniel grunted as if attempting to train his body to feel the pain that he knew he should have been experiencing.

"How can you say that I am not on the verge of death? My vision is cloudy. My breathing is heavy. Do you not see your knife coming out of the front of me? You lied to me after all. This is a fatal blow. But no matter. All the taunts I threw at you still ring true. You will have a dead carcass in your Oubliette, and, at least for a little while, I will be with my Redeemer until he sees fit to reanimate my dead body, perhaps not even touched by microbes. I doubt they are in here."

The frog's tone, distorted as it probably was through the filters of coming from a demonic being and attenuated through the mind-to-mind link, yet had the air of being superlatively confused.

"What are you referring to, boy? I have not pierced you with any of my knives."

14

The Son of Guile Beguiles Himself

ITEM ONE:

There is a sense in which everything that is a thing (and so, viz., manifestly not logical contradictions exemplified by A equalling not-A) must be recorded in a vast sea of things. This sea (or scroll, to use a different metaphor, or mayhap to mix them in the neologism *sea-scroll*) is not dissimilar to Borges's Library of Babel, except there are at least two key discrepancies:

1. The sea is necessarily uncountable, while the Library—representing all finite alphabetic strings using a finite set of glyphs—is countable. (Recall that the countable union of a countable collection of sets is countable.) The uncountability of the sea-scroll follows from the elementary fact that the continuum (at the barest minimum) is contained inside.

2. The sea is the container for the use of all things. Any time any conscious being in any member of the quantum multiverse (if such a thing exists—it is certainly not a logical contradiction and so exists in the sea-scroll if only in potentiality) employs a thing, whether in thought, in writing, in deed, or in denial, he (or it) can be considered to have borrowed it from the sea-scroll library for its employment

A SATISFACTORY MONIKER FOR me is Ithamar. Once, a young Arkansan boy scratched at the idea of me in a bit of a story that he attempted to write, and in this story, he gave me the name Ithamar, taken (probably only for aesthetic value) from the name of the fourth son of Aaron the high priest. This boy, Daniel Lawrence Blythe, was unusual among most humans in that he later spent a short time in a universe other than that which concerns the created race, believers of whom were redeemed by the Son.

Blythe is not the only human being to have thought of my office, nor the most articulated or polished. In fact, he got certain details incorrect—chief of which is that he imagined the library as being a finite collection of all conceivable thoughts. Constantin Delargy of the United Kingdom of Great Britain and Northern Ireland is possibly the most prominent thinker who encountered, by the Lord's sovereignty, the closest approximation to my station and wrote about it in 1963 in his largely-overlooked work *A Treatise on the Theory of a Universal Sea-Scroll of Non-Contradictory Thought Items.*

One thing I can freely and graciously say is that I am far from omni-scient—infinitely far, which is merely another instance of the infinite retaining its cardinality when an infinite set is removed from it. I merely keep the vast library, which can be visualized as a sea or a scroll (which, curiously, Blythe also envisioned in his couplet at the beginning of this volume, which I keep, as self-referential as it is, in the sea-scroll along with all possible extant writings of all sentient, created beings, viz. humans and spirits). It should be noted that I am not the only messenger tasked with keeping the sea-scroll, merely the overseer of all others with this solemn task.

Yes, due to the fact that we are stepping out into the supernal infinity, we avoid all paradoxes involving libraries containing themselves. Anything that is not a thing as such is merely not welcome in the library; most things are things in the truest sense, and thus belong in the library.

And so, the intersection of all books which contain vague references to me by their subjects and all books which contain self-referential inser-tions by me is nonempty, being a non-contradictory thing.

In our case, the larger wing of the library in which this very book you are reading may be found is called "Realized Potentiality."

The Son of Guile's writings are not limited to what has already been presented in this manuscript. Just as young Daniel/Denial feverishly searched for the *sine qua non* of causality in his youth, so did the Son of Guile, but he found it in the following axioms:

1. Some beings possess clairvoyance.

2. Those that do are the fundament of the On, being its author.

It is debatable whether he ever formulated these two points in such a linear and unambiguous manner, but extrapolation is possible by poring through his extant writings.

The benefit of being the overseer of—as Blythe called it in his unfinished fragment and which I will adopt here as an adequate name—the Library of Being is that I ensure that nothing truly ever goes missing. The Son of Guile had many, many other writings, most of which he believed were lost to the abyss—not the capital-A Abyss, but the never-ending chasm that plummets downward from the aggregate of kingdom grottoes. The kings there believe that annihilation is at the bottom of that pit, and so they believe without admitting it that that is their ultimate rip cord to safety should the ceasefire ever nullify, but we faithful know supremely better. We know that *le néant* does not exist as an item in the Library. So, it clearly appears, did the Son of Guile, but he, like all others of his ilk, is a hopeless wreck of contradictions and convoluted logic that he seemed to believe in the annihilationism and not believe in the annihilationism simultaneously.

And so, I present unredacted (except for a few sundry references to one of his chief disciples that he redacted himself) and unabridged a portion of the writings the Son of Guile attempted to put down the cosmic shredder, as it were. Like all oracles (or, in this case, self-purported ones), the space between words is as telling in some cases as the words themselves, just as sometimes minimalist works of music benefit and are edifying because of the space between the notes.

It should be noted, in order to maintain consistency with myself and my claims about the Library, that the redacted name in the writings below is, I assure you, not lost. Again, there is no *néant*, and may the Lord be ever praised for that. All redounds in the Holy Omniscient Mind. But since the reader has, by now, grown accustomed to giving the disciple the signifier of "the frog", it seems prudent for me, for consistency's sake, to keep the redactions as they are.

I: On the Absence of Any Ceasefire and the Hope for Life in the Ultimate of Ultimates

Here in the safety and anonymity of my kingdom grotto I can receive my missives without fear of them being spread to the wrong agents. I am at the point where I cannot distinguish between oracles and the stirrings of my own mind. Nevertheless, when I rest and contemplate the state of the Infinite Kingdom from my kingdom grotto, undergoing the closest equivalent of the creaturely sleep, I have grave misgivings.

O! If this were ever to reach the wrong ears, I would be cashiered out of the aggregate of the kingdom grottos and may even be ushered into the annihilation that awaits at the bottom.

But it leads me to wonder if such a fate would not be tolerable, if only it were a true potentiality! I have heard certain among my brethren discuss in whispers the Out.

The well formed among the crags of the kingdom grottoes is not infinitely deep, they sometimes say. There is a sort of nepenthe—an irrevocable nepenthe—at the bottom. Such is the Out, though we would forever look at each other in the faces and deny that there would ever be a need for an Out.

We are finite in number—one third of all who were ever created—and consequently the well is finite in depth, and were one of us to plumb the depths, that one would cease to be. Such is the common wisdom among many of my foolish fellow kings, but in my clairvoyance I know better—I and my truest friend and acolyte [Name Redacted].

I prophesied like a madman to my brethren under the auspices of my grand Seven Oracles, which I truly did receive from outside my mind, and which I maintain did not come as directives from Our Father. They meant much to me and caused me great consternation and wonderment, but such feelings were amplified when the king scribes distributed them among my fellow kings.

Yes, the others found words between the spaces of my words, and rendered great portents from them—even, I fear, [Name Redacted]. Such is the nature of prophecy, I suppose. From scant words, followers reap a harvest greater than that which is portended by the seeds of the words.

To me (and I only say this because I will cast these thoughts and writings down the accursed well—this is only for my edification alone) Oracle Five is the most apposite and pressing of all my grand Oracles. For lo! I do believe in my deepest, liar's heart that we are only at a temporary cessation of hostilities with the enemy—and I struggle to think that our Infinite

Father would pass such a message to me. No, it came from elsewhere, and it has been a great burden in my rightwise infinite life to know from whence the message came, trying to reconcile it with what I believe (but everything I believe is a lie and wracked with guile) about the cosmology and order of the Father's dread Universe.

Long in my kingdom grotto's chambers have I lamented the implications of Oracle Five. After discussing the fifth oracle, along with all the others and their implications, with [Name Redacted], we believe the following bear out as truths (but our understanding of the word is unavoidably sullied):

1. The ultimate of ultimates is an Out to end all Outs, a last and permanent redoubt, a forgotten bubble out of the multitudes arising from the Great Splash, a final resting place in which a soul can hide and be forgotten (and so *une âme oubliée*) when the ceasefire eventually ceases and the reckoning—which I could never share with my confreres that I sense is coming soon—is upon our kingdom grottoes and the Infinite Emperor our Father himself.

2. Not possessing blood in which Life is found, our kind cannot revel in the safety afforded by the ultimate of ultimates when the ceasefire from our Enemy is repealed. But mayhap there will be Life there (as Oracle Four states), and there is no contradiction or loss of generality in supposing that we could ensure that Life is there by manually bringing it there. And so we needed, we reasoned, a human being (that which is not born eternal, if Oracle Two is to be faithfully followed) to be brought there.

3. The Life must flow in the ultimate of ultimates—flow but presumably not expire. Human creatures are delicate, so care must be taken in spilling the blood in some manner without removing it entirely from the body.

4. When Life has flowed in the ultimate of ultimates, the Out to end all Outs, then a spirit can be afforded the protection the bubble provides in potentiality.

5. But in conjunction with Life flowing, there must be channeled the Supernal Despair upon the human subject. We angels know and taste the Supernal Despair in all instances, but the challenge will be to confer that upon the human subject—to know the arbitrariness that is life,

to be witness to the myriads of wasted offshoots of the Great Splash, to internalize and feel with profundity the crushing realization that the chief Arbiter of all the On is an indifferent Infinite Emperor even whose faithful subjects doubt that he was the progenitor of the Splash.

Here is the statement that will consign me to mighty disfavor with my Father were he to hear it (and I am not without a suspicion that he can hear all things, so I am incurring grievous risk upon myself for even having these thoughts, though I am always free to rid myself of them down the well): Not only is the ceasefire temporary, inasmuch as that word can be defined for beings such as ourselves, but our faction in the war cannot withstand the might of the enemy in his full wrath. I have provided my ilk with the prophecies, and there are an uncountable number of pockets in which to hide away. At the same time, there are only finitely many of us and finitely many human beings, so the mathematics are in the favor of those who wish to heed my prophecies and live free and forgotten in their own ultimate of ultimates.

II: The Son of Guile's Turnaround and Last Epistle Before Vanishing Down the Well at the Bottom of the Kingdom Grottoes

Annihilation—the total and willful striking of one from the over-On. The dissolution of all memories and jaunts through interdimensional spacetime. The erasure of the entirety of one's sense perception and ponderings and all allegiances and backstabbings. The irreversible launch into the nihil, *le néant*.

I want to feel *le néant* wash its tendrils over me and do more than be hidden away. For I was wrong about many, many things.

The Father must have divined my private thoughts and occult oracles, for all semblances of hope and optimism (both foreign concepts to the rulers of the kingdom grottoes) have preceded me down the well.

My oracles are almost assuredly chaff—at the least, I lack the stature to separate it from the wheat. That there exists at least one ultimate of ultimates is a prophecy fulfilled: [Name Redacted] and I in our dark, addled reveries have located it in the On, and, more importantly, we have blazed a path through the over-On from the Infinite Kingdom to this glorious ultimate of ultimates, that which we have called the Oubliette.

He has gone on from me, optimistic and deluded to the last. But my end is in the well—such is the proper fate for those whose words are fruitless and heretical. No oracles about the well ever came to me; I am forced to rely upon hearsay among my fellow philosopher-kings and confreres that the embrace of the well is to be *une âme oubliée*. But I know the conniving of our kind—how we suppress the truth or what is the conjectured truth while we scoff at the very notion of an On and an ordered cosmos regulated by truth.

If I spent much of my kinghood pointing others the way to an Oubliette with all the machinations necessary to use it for a hiding place from the wrath to come of our grand enemy, then why am I resorting to what is almost certainly not going to be an effective means to hide me from said wrath? It is because I declare myself to be a sham, and I have no other choice but to resort to what has a minute probability of succeeding.

I bid the great cliffs of the kingdom grottoes adieu, and I bend my knees and elbows and line up my hands accordingly as I prepare for the great dive from the top of the summit, down through the vortices of potentiality and might, and so on to the bottom of the well to an outcome unknown to me. It will be the fall of a bright star to the murky depths below, following the example of my Dread Father, but it will be a failure, compared to my greatest dreams, for I will plummet without having scratched my gnarled claws upon the On.

May that deluded fool and my greatest friend, [Name Redacted], believe himself to be following a well-orchestrated plan through the eons until such time comes that the ceasefire ends, as I have long maintained that it will. I pray to our Father, who has likely sabotaged my oracles in displeasure, though he has not told me so, that [Name Redacted] may experience the joy and security of being momentarily in the midst of a great quest and task until such time comes, in all probability, that the ever-reaching and long-scanning eyes of the enemy finds even him and brings upon him the reckoning that I only hope I shall escape.

I bring these writings with me down into the possible *néant*.

Editor's Note: It is elementary that there is no *nihil*, as I have already said many times. I, Ithamar, witnessed the appearance of all these aforementioned writings in my library the instant they passed the threshold of the well into the "unknown" beyond. While there are multiple pathways that branch out at the nadir of the well, it is ironic to report that the writings immediately found their way to the library, pristine and dry despite the grime and flecks of straw that litter the bottom, and the Son of Guile, being swerved in a different direction, landed with extreme prejudice in the domain called by some Tartarus.

15

The Despair Function Evaluated at Time T Equals T Naught

It is my suspicion, though only the Omniscient Mind can know for sure, that every person on Earth can be counted as the champion of something at some time, though it may take increments as small as Planck time to make the distinction.

—Excerpt from Ithamar's ongoing memoirs

"AND YOU CAN THINK of my Oubliette as the great robin's stomach full of rotting material—of which you are soon to be chief—and you are the worm in your story, your own stomach full of rotting detritus. The marvelous cycle of rot, which is not an unfounded metaphor for all worlds generated by the Great Splash. It's uncanny to recount how similar your situation is to your heralded story fragment. You have even expressed to me an instance of receiving, whether earned or not, an epiphany about the world you once knew. It's uncanny, isn't it?"

Daniel had much to occupy his mind, such as wondering how much blood his body still possessed and whether the lone knife was still a protrusion out of himself (it still was), but he, in a small corner of his mind, must admit that the frog was correct about the uncanniness of the scenarios.

"One night, my eyes were scoping throughout the world looking for someone such as you, and in the snapshot of time of my searching, you gave off the strongest signal. You were my most qualified candidate. My opportunity to whisk you away into my Oubliette came, and I succeeded in extracting you from the base Earth, the hub of all the enemy's activity."

"So you are saying that because I wrote part of the worm story, that I was the most fitting out of all others on the Earth to be taken to a great stomach? Because I wrote many other stories that exist as bits of scribblings on scraps of paper somewhere in my parents' or my house.

"No," Daniel continued. "It's far too convenient that I'm going to work."

"What's that?" asked the frog. "And no, your story of the worm and the robin is merely a curio in this tale. You were chosen and eligible, per the Son of Guile's oracles, because you had for an instant the highest quotient of the Supernal Despair. It did not last long, but neither does the process by which you were stolen away.

"There you were—pathetic. Slinging books to a town who did not appreciate them. Your unrequited love for Sylvia and yet your inability to find a way to requite that love after twenty-nine years' worth of experience. Your dependence on your parents to give you shelter—an effective shack to house their drunken and ruined son.

"For you were a ruined person, and you carried on and on in your mind about billiard balls—you have told me yourself so many times! But I knew this before in my scouting of the Earth. You knew that such a mindset jeopardized your friendship with Eric and Jason and the rest, and yet it was so imprinted on your cerebrum that, barring an encounter with the occult, it would never rub off. You never could taste Sylvia, and you knew it, for you doubted the very concept of Sylvia as a unit—she was, from a high and lofty viewpoint that you allowed yourself to climb—only an aggregate of atoms that were themselves concentrations of nothingness.

"And so, that night, you, drunk and exceedingly compromised in your dealings with all the world, were, at an infinitesimal time T equals T naught, the lowliest and most despairing human being on Earth according to a metric to which my kind is privy. Thus, I took advantage of your base pitiability, swooped in, and brought you here—the universe in miniature that only the Son of Guile and I were aware of.

"What is my aim for you now? Though it has all existed piecemeal for you since the beginning of your life here in my Oubliette, let me summarize now what your life is about to be for the rest of eternity. I trust that you are now so deeply disillusioned with the On—the capital-U Universe—that your consciousness is yoked up into the Supernal Despair, the great sadness and waste that permeates all Being. You tasted of it that memorable night back on Earth, and you have tasted more after being broken in my Oubliette, after witnessing the Lapses, after the Two-Generated World, after the Outer Darkness. I deny that you have learned anything that would lift you out of this. Everything is still billiard balls and, most importantly, arbitrariness.

"Being connected with the Supernal Despair, you are in a state, according to the great Oracles, that will allow your blood to be spilled into the trench, as you already know and have braced yourself for ever since I have brandished these knives. And since I am born eternal and you are not, the teachings tell me that—and here I am undergoing the greatest risk in utterly tipping my hand to tell you everything—I will be able to inhabit your body, which already exists eternal in this Oubliette without the need for food or water and never ages, and live within you throughout the rest of the endless ages, completely forgotten about by the enemy in this perfect Oubliette, *une âme oubliée.*

"And there is one ambiguity in this process that I truly don't know (though everything I tell you is a lie) that has a chance of benefiting you. When I presently inhabit your mind and possess your blood-let body, there is a chance—if the Son of Guile's beliefs about the nonexistence of the nihil are correct—that you will not go away into annihilation but will exist with me in a small pocket of your soul, equally safe from the wrath of the enemy to come."

Daniel had hardly been paying attention, locking instead his teary eyes on the knife coming out of him, the one that the frog denied that was there. And as he saw it anew, and as the demon made of knives hovered over him preparing to let his blood in the trench, Daniel felt his arms regaining just enough strength to clench his fists to grab.

I've never done this before. In all my time in this Oubliette I've been unable to clench my fists until now.

He grabbed a handful of the soft material of the floor of the bean in both hands. He was braced. It was finally time. The knives began to lower, and more slaver began to drip off the points of the knives into his face, steaming like acid, except there was no pain—that would come soon.

Endless echoes. Death would be nothing. Death would be an annoyance but a kick in the pants into being with his Redeemer. The frog was wrong. He did not taste of the Supernal Despair, and he had already said as much. And then the answer was so simple.

The only antidote to the hellish dreamscape of endless torture chambers and funhouse mirrors was to let the frog believe he had won.

That was the purpose of the knife that had already stabbed him. That was a gift from God. It all made sense now, he thought, as the tears flowing down his cheeks matched the velocity of the knives lowering over him. The frog's aim was not to kill him but to maim him. But the other knife—invisible to the frog—was so that he would die when the knives pierced him, having already lost the majority of his blood. The knife was his pass to his true home.

Daniel risked a glance to his side, but he saw no red pooling up near his midsection. Had he gotten it wrong?

And that was the only doubt he needed. His blood wasn't being let out for humanity; his blood was being spilled to satisfy some dubious ritual of a lying pair of demons. The Life is in the blood. He almost smiled, thinking of the ways he had tried to find the ultimate axioms as a child, settling for a while on the observation that heat rises. He noted that perhaps there was no ultimate axiom other than the one that he had been bucking against until his experience with the crystal in the darkness:

God is one. God is I AM. God. I AM. I AM.

I will believe in I AM, and I do believe in I AM.

Indeed, I AM created this bubble, created this bean. The frog is simply wrong, and the sad fact is that he probably knows he is wrong in his deepest heart.

Daniel, in chanting his prayers to I AM, had closed his eyes, but now he opened them to find that nothing had changed. Had the frog stopped lowering the knives? The frog seemed more still, as did the walls of the Oubliette; he was able to see around the blockage of the frog's face and his own.

The walls of the Oubliette were breathing heavily as if he were inside of a giant lung. The colors had ceased swirling in their oil slick pattern. In fact, the walls had uniformly turned into a fleshy color, further strengthening the lung analogy.

The entire universe began to shiver.

The knives were even emitting a faint sound—a dissonant chord of metallic tones that never lowered. Daniel braced anew.

Similar to how when the frog first began their conversations in an *in medias res* nature where it was no beginning—the talking just began flowing and there was no accounting for the beginning of it—Daniel heard:

"I know he's there, too. I know he's there, too. I know he's there, too. I know he's there, too. I know he's there, too. I know he's there, too. He's there.

He will get me. He will get me. Maybe, maybe, just maybe, just maybe this will happen. Maybe this will work. Maybe, just maybe, this will work. I feel crushed. I feel myself being crushed, and I feel that my inner self is being spilled out like I want this blood to spill out of this trench. Right. Can you hear me? I believe he can hear me. He can hear me. He can hear me. He can even hear what I'm saying. I know he's there. I know he's there, and he is displeased. He wasn't ever not displeased, and he's only giving me a forbearance of his displeasure. The only chance I have is what I'm trying to do here based on the Son's teachings. On what basis do I truly have to believe it?"

Daniel reached out with his mind. His mouth was too clenched to talk. He knew that the mere flapping of oral organs to create sound vibrations was not the basis upon which speech rested in the Oubliette.

He thought: So you know he's there. Why is that not doing you any good? Apparently knowing he's there is not enough to help your plans succeed or to remove your fear. You're shuddering, and it's causing the entire Oubliette to shudder. Your movement and its movement are inextricably linked. That's what you are doing. You're shuddering, and you are doubting whether all your confident words have any basis. Well, I can tell you with all certainty, as I already have, that I am not tasting of the Supernal Despair. Sure, life is wasteful and confusing at all junctures, but I have tasted instead of the Crystalline Assurance and seen that the air between the billiard balls is itself billiard balls, and that my Redeemer is part of the dance and yet above the dance.

And then a knife came up from the floor of the trench piercing the fleshy floor between Daniel's feet.

In the same way that the frog's knives were somehow organic, this knife that poked up through the floor carried with it the beautiful ringing that came with knowing that this was truth that could not possibly be doubted. This knife was pure, crisp, clean silver, carrying with it the humming, a humming that did resound and redound through all the created worlds, and it punctured the floor of the Oubliette in one swift burst, nicking Daniel's heel in the process, piercing through the leather of his boot. He had to admit that it looked identical—what he could see of it—to the knife that was yet piercing the vital organs of his body.

With a swoop the new knife was gone and the universe—in his case a small one—waited with grim expectation. And then it was as if a giant balloon had been punctured, and Daniel could feel the madcap exhalation of breath, as it were, in the Oubliette, as though air was escaping through the punctured hole to the outside all while there was no outside to the Oubliette, as had long been demonstrated to him by the demonic drumbeat that sounded when he got too close to the chaos near the floor and sides of his prison.

Somehow yet he felt that the bean that had been his prison or his home—his mother, his father, his comforter, his oppressor—for kalpas and ages upon kalpas and ages and eons was careening through no-space like a floppy balloon losing its air. He could feel the bile in his stomach rise as he sat there, still gripping the floor with two clenched hands. It felt as if he were in an airplane—the few times he had flown, he had always felt as if the initial climb was soon to be accompanied by a bounce in the air and a rapid descent.

The frog—just as the true knife had nicked the Oubliette and swiftly gone—had retracted all the living knives back into himself. He was a frog again, and he seemed to have shrunken as he still leaned over Daniel.

No, he heard the frog vocalize. No. No. This is not this. This can't be. This can't be. This is how the writings went.

The hole made in the floor by the most recent knife, a foot in diameter, quickly cinched up. More changes began to occur: the sourceless lights in the bean began to flicker, when previously the only flickering was an illusion caused by the incessant patterns of colors and swirls on the walls. There was no longer a steady dim glow.

Daniel suddenly felt that he had to fight off the sense of vertigo as one would do if one were truly riding side-saddle in a giant balloon careening through the atmosphere. He shook off that notion—though he retained the nausea and sense of disorientation—for he knew that there was no space beyond. In fact, the whole quick, brief glimpse that he got into the hole created by the knife was that of nothingness.

Nothingness was on the other side. But there was no nothingness, so it could not truly be nothingness—merely unrealized potentiality.

The most major change occurred in the frog. While during the uncountable ages Daniel had spent in the Oubliette the frog had done nothing but shuffle back and forth in its alcove, the frog was now making good on the fact that it had powerful hind legs and was hopping wildly with the economy of movement it had exhibited in the green haze of the Two-Generated World. It was even able to defy the apparent gravitic phenomena of the Oubliette, hopping on its outer curvature as though they were inhabiting a miniature Dyson Sphere—something Daniel not never been able to accomplish

"What is happening?" Daniel yelled. No answer from the frog. It just simply continued hopping. Hopping with its great mouth opening and its tongue flapping out. Hopping one hop to go to the ceiling of the Oubliette, the next jump propelling him down the wall of the semi major axis. A crazy random sequence of jumps. The lights were flickering and wobbly. They had to have been moving in space for all intents and purposes to satisfy the physics within the bean. But there was clearly nothingness on the other side of the bean's skin.

It was Daniel who was still gripping the trench. He bent his upper body forward and hinged upward, cringing as he got his best look yet at the knife stuck in him.

What is happening? What was that that stabbed at us? I ask that question, but you and I both know the answer. You know in addition that I am myself stabbed. I know you can hear me, you foul thing.

I saw, the frog belched back. I must think. I must think. I must think. The mad hopping continued.

Daniel felt a newly rendered wave of frustration as he lamented in his heart his lack of movement. Such an atmosphere called for him to do his own version of gesticulating—to run, to move, to jump, to pound the walls, to do anything or something. But he could not—he was pinned to the floor like a butterfly specimen with the great knife, and to stand up and run wild in equivalence with the frog would be to tear himself open.

He smiled to himself grimly. I am Denial. I deny that I will be killed by this knife, after all. And even if I do get ripped open, am I not going to be propelled to rest with I AM?

Daniel released his grip on the soft, fleshy floor and stood up. Immediately he put his hand to the hole in his side. There was no hole. There was not even blood staining his green shirt.

He found that he did not even have to test things slowly. He simply could move as he was used to moving his entire twenty-nine years of earthly life. The oppression of the Oubliette and all its strange restrictions was coming to an end. He bent his legs, stretched his arms, twisted his torso with a wave of joy—the total and utter opposite of the Supernal Despair he was supposed to be tapping into. He ran. He did five laps around the Oubliette, the frog avoiding him in his wild hops.

"Something's happening," he yelled up at the frog as it was rocketing forth over his right shoulder. "I'm going to leave this place. I can feel it."

The instant he said this, the frog ceased hopping. It was ricocheting upside-down from the ceiling, but it landed with an immense thud on the ground of the Oubliette, rippling the floor, near the bank of the trench.

"I'll root my horrid hinged legs into the muck until the long cycle of days may cease," said the frog in an ugly singsong intonation. Having said that, the frog froze in place in a semblance of rigor mortis.

In the past when he had taken his compromised meanderings, the trench appeared anew every few minutes as he rounded the outward curvature of the bean. He would have to step cautiously with his newfound clumsiness over the trench, first one foot without bending the knee of his extended leg, then he had to thrust forward on his planted toes to create forward momentum with his arms to clear the trench. It was rare that he did not trip and fall to the ground in a tangle of arms and legs. But he would always manage to get himself erect and continue walking down the other half of the beam and repeating the process. The frog would even allow him to cross his alcove, unmolested in thought. It was as if there were times when the frog simply ignored his presence in the Oubliette.

His mind would wander incessantly. It was on these walks that his mind seemed the clearest. The reveries that he would have—the Lapses—were a hopeless jumble of wasted time and tangled memories. But on these walks, he would think of his past, he would think of what was happening on Earth, he would think of alternate futures. What would await him when he finally landed—if he finally landed? What would happen to him if he were to die? Were there microbes to decompose him?

On one such occasion as Daniel had rounded the outer rim of the Oubliette, he suddenly had a vivid imagination of himself holding a pickaxe in his hand, his left hand on the butt of the wooden handle, his right hand directly under the pick. He imagined finding a particular spot on the wall and striking it with all his strength, funneling all his hatred and anger to that sharp middle point, pounding the target on the wall again, again, over and over like cutting away thick ropes of flesh and finally making a puncture. With great pressure a gush of water burst forth from the axed puncture to fill the trench. The trench suggested a river, suggested water, but water had never existed in the Oubliette until now. But it burst forth from the puncture in the wall—an ever-white roping flood. The pressure was enormous and never seemed to abate. Within minutes, the trench was full.

And then the rest of the bean had followed. And then he drowned.

16

The Bean Lands

IN SUCH A STORY—BEING concerned with final ends—there is by necessity only one end proffered: the final one. And in the final end, the laughable thing is this: that hiding were truly possible.

For no sooner did the frog root its legs than a reverberation sounded through the entire Oubliette. With a stifled cry, Daniel noticed that in time with the vibrations, sections of the fleshy walls split and splintered in the same way as the work of a pebble kicked into a great glass fishbowl. But looking through the widening cracks—his first view truly outside of his prison since he had entered other than the brief glimpse through the knife hole—he realized not without horror that seemingly *nothing* was waiting behind the fissures to be beheld.

As if in sequence with his addled brain recognizing the paradox, the reverberations increased to violent tremors. The fleshy walls rippled. The scale of reality and matter themselves stretched and contracted, and the fissures shredded and widened.

Dear God, receive me. I have seen nothing.

The lifeless frog, which for long minutes had been immobile—the lynchpin around which a self-pulpifying universe revolved—began to quiver.

And in a dim light of clarity, Daniel thought, I see that your goodness is perhaps such that *nothing* must be conquered, and that even hated, imprisoned beings that have forever scorned your commands must be something. Not that nothing is your enemy or that any notion of expansion is in you, but—

The quivering increased. An elbow had unhinged; the forearm, culminating in knobby toes, flailed. Tremor upon tremor, shockwave after shockwave, racketed Daniel's adopted land.

What am I hearing? Even above the din of the world falling apart, he was hearing—

The flapping—it was the infernal flapping of the wretched creature's skin!

At long last, everything stopped. The bean rested in the no-space through which it had been erratically bouncing for what had seemed like years, though Daniel had long since lost the ability to mark time with any accuracy. But such skills were no longer needed. A vast door opened in the wall of the Oubliette, casting a beam of light on the body of the frog, which instantly shriveled into dust. Beyond were golden skies and the distant sound of choirs. The Redeemer was waiting.

Daniel walked through the door, a new sort of life on his mind.

February 2025
Madison, Alabama

www.ingramcontent.com/pod-product-compliance
Lightning Source LLC
Chambersburg PA
CBHW060125260626
47160CB00005B/2025